What have we done?

I shot Salvador a glance and caught him staring at me again. He quickly looked away, pretending to be very interested in his carton of juice. I stared down at my sandwich and gulped.

Maybe kissing Salvador was an even bigger mistake than I realized, I thought. Taking a bite of my sandwich, I glanced at Anna out of the corner of my eye. Her face looked thoughtful and sort of sad, and she was totally oblivious to my gaze, like she wasn't even at the table with us. *Or like she wishes she weren't,* I thought with a sinking sensation. *If Salvador and I don't figure out how to stick to just being friends, we might both lose Anna forever.*

Don't miss any of the books in SWEET VALLEY JUNIOR HIGH, an exciting new series from Bantam Books!

How to Ruin a Friendship

Written by
Jamie Suzanne

Created by
FRANCINE PASCAL

BANTAM BOOKS
NEW YORK • TORONTO • LONDON • SYDNEY • AUCKLAND

RL 4, 008-012

HOW TO RUIN A FRIENDSHIP
A Bantam Book / August 1999

Sweet Valley Junior High is a trademark of
Francine Pascal.

Conceived by Francine Pascal.

Produced by 17th Street Productions,
a division of Daniel Weiss Associates, Inc.
33 West 17th Street, New York, NY 10011.

ISBN: 0-553-48619-5

Published simultaneously in the United States and Canada

Bantam Books are published by Bantam Books, a division of Random
House, Inc. Its trademark, consisting of the words "Bantam Books" and
the portrayal of a rooster, is Registered in the U.S. Patent and Trademark
Office and in other countries. Marca Registrada. Bantam Books, 1540
Broadway, New York, New York 10036.

PRINTED IN THE UNITED STATES OF AMERICA

OPM   0 9 8 7 6 5 4 3 2 1

To Juliette Daviron

Elizabeth

"Elizabeth! Over here!" Salvador del Valle called the minute I entered the Sweet Valley Junior High cafeteria. He waved me over to our usual table, where he and Anna Wang were sitting side by side. As I got closer, I saw that Salvador had peeled back the top layer of his tuna sandwich and was loading it with handfuls of crushed potato chips. Anna was staring into her bowl of split-pea soup, probably wondering what had possessed her to buy it. At least that's what I would have been wondering if I were her. It only took me one day of eating the toxic sludge the cafeteria called lunch to learn to brown-bag it. I hurried over, dropped my lunch bag on the table, and sat down in the empty seat next to Anna's.

"Hi, Elizabeth." Salvador smiled at me from across the table, wiping the potato-chip grease off his fingers by rubbing them on his algebra book. "It's a good thing they don't give detentions for being late to lunch, or you'd be totally busted."

Elizabeth

"Very funny," I said, shifting in my chair. I was really only a couple of minutes late, if even. Was Salvador *that* conscious of every moment I wasn't around? "I was just talking to Brian at our locker. About the 'zine article."

At the beginning of the school year Anna, Salvador, and I had joined the staff of the *Spectator,* the official school newspaper. But it hadn't taken us long to realize that the editors took their jobs—and themselves—way too seriously. That's when the three of us decided to start our own 'zine called *Zone.* And then our friend Brian Rainey had offered to help too. We figured we'd have a lot more fun than we would pretending we worked for *The Wall Street Journal*—or as Salvador would say, *The Dull Street Journal.*

"So when are you and Brian going to check out Sweet Valley's answer to the Space Needle?" Salvador wiggled his eyebrows. "I hope neither of you is afraid of heights over six feet, or you're in trouble."

One of our regular features was going to be a column called "Heights and Sights." Brian Rainey and I planned to review all sorts of interesting places around the area. We were starting with the Sweet Valley Tower, the tallest structure in town.

I giggled. "I think we'll be okay. But I'll be sure to warn Brian. We're going tonight right after dinner. It's supposed to be a full moon, and we thought it would be fun to call the article 'Sweet Valley by Moonlight' or something like that." I shrugged. "Actually, it was Brian's idea."

Brian is my locker partner, and—according to my twin sister, Jessica—one of the coolest guys in the entire school. Jessica is constantly trying to bribe me to switch locker partners. Her latest offer was to let me read all her new fashion magazines first for a whole month, which for her would be a major sacrifice. Her locker partner, Ronald Rheece, is perfectly nice, but he isn't exactly the most popular guy in school.

"I can probably turn out a draft of the article by our meeting tomorrow if I get all my homework done first," I continued, unwrapping my sandwich. As I raised it to my mouth to take a bite, I happened to glance across the table. Salvador was staring at me, his black eyes totally focused and serious, as if he was hanging on my every word.

As soon as he saw that I'd caught him, he looked away quickly and started talking about how the Sweet Valley Tower was probably the shortest tower in the world and how it would take about a thousand of them to equal the Eiffel

Tower in Paris or the Sears Tower in Chicago or any other self-respecting tower anywhere in the world. But I noticed that his cheeks were turning kind of pink as he talked.

I wonder if Anna noticed too, I thought uneasily.

Before this year, when Jessica and I got transferred from Sweet Valley Middle School to Sweet Valley Junior High, I never knew that making two amazing new friends could make my life so complicated. I mean, I definitely never expected that I would start having all these weird feelings for Salvador.

But somehow things got tangled up almost from the beginning, ever since the time Salvador asked me out on a date when he'd already made plans to hang out with Anna at the same time. That night was still kind of a touchy subject for the three of us.

I guess maybe that's why neither Salvador nor I was eager to discuss what happened at the party Jessica and I threw at our house not long ago. I could barely keep myself from blushing as I flashed back to that moment in my brother's room. My fingers clenched against my palms under the table as I remembered how it had felt when Salvador kissed me. *Stop it,* I told myself sternly. Thinking about that kiss right in front of Anna felt incredibly wrong somehow. *Maybe because she and Salvador have been best friends forever and she has a right to know what happened,* I thought angrily. But neither Salvador nor I had the guts to tell her.

I glanced over at Anna, suddenly realizing that she hadn't said anything at all since I sat down.

Her long, beautiful black hair was hanging straight down, brushing against the table and hiding most of her face from my view. She was staring into her soup and stirring it slowly, moving her spoon around and around.

"Did you forget your lunch today, Anna?" I asked, trying to sound casual but unable to keep my voice from squeaking.

She didn't answer. She just kept on stirring. Stirring. Stirring.

I cleared my throat. "Hey, Anna," I said, raising my voice a little. "Anna?"

Finally she looked up. Her big, dark eyes blinked twice. "Huh?"

"Earth to Anna!" Salvador covered his mouth with his hand and made static sounds, pretending to be mission control. "Earth to Anna! Come in, please!"

Anna pushed her hair behind her ear and gazed at both of us. "I'm sorry. What did you say?"

"It's all right," I said, deciding to let the soup

thing drop. "We were just talking about my article. I hope I can get it done by tomorrow."

"Oh." Anna blinked again. "That's good. Which article?"

"The one about the Tower." I gave her a careful look, noticing how her eyes didn't seem to focus. "Are you all right?" I asked. "You're acting kind of . . . distracted."

She shrugged her slender shoulders. "I'm just a little tired, I guess."

Without another word, she returned her gaze to her soup, staring into the bowl as if the smushed peas and little chunks of hamlike stuff held the secret to the meaning of life.

Salvador and I exchanged a puzzled look. Anna was definitely acting weird. And now that I thought about it, she'd been kind of quiet and moody for a couple of days now.

I hope she's okay, I thought worriedly. My heart almost stopped as another possibility occurred to me. *I hope she hasn't noticed what's going on between me and Salvador. Whatever it is anyway.*

I shot Salvador a glance and caught him staring at me again. He quickly looked away, pretending to be very interested in his carton of juice. I stared down at my sandwich and gulped.

Maybe kissing Salvador was an even bigger mistake than I realized, I thought. Taking a bite of my sandwich, I glanced at Anna out of the corner of my eye. Her face looked thoughtful and sort of sad, and she was totally oblivious to my gaze, like she wasn't even at the table with us. *Or like she wishes she weren't,* I thought with a sinking sensation. *If Salvador and I don't figure out how to stick to just being friends, we might both lose Anna forever.*

Jessica

I am way too nice for my own good.

There I was, just standing at the end of the lunch line, waiting to buy juice. Minding my own business. Wondering if my English teacher was actually *trying* to kill us all by assigning forty-two pages of reading that week, and if so, if I could turn her in for attempted murder.

That was when the commotion started up at the front of the line. There was a huge crash, and then several people, including the lunch lady at the cash register, started shouting. Most of them sounded pretty annoyed.

I craned my neck, trying to see what was happening. All I could tell was that everyone was gathered around a spot right in front of the register. And that the line had totally stopped.

"What's going on?" I asked the guy in front of me.

He shrugged and stepped out of the line to get a better look. I still couldn't see a thing— there were way too many people milling around up there. But the guy in front of me was pretty tall, so I guess he had a better view.

After a second he stepped back into line. "It's nothing," he said with a snort. "It's just that nerd Rheece falling over his big feet again."

I rolled my eyes. *I should have known,* I thought. *The dorkiest locker partner in the universe strikes again.*

A moment later the crowd parted a little, and I could see for myself exactly what had happened. Ronald Rheece was sitting on the floor near the cash register in the middle of what remained of his lunch. His brown hair stuck up even more than usual, and his skinny little legs were splayed out in a puddle of the revolting pea soup that had started out in his bowl.

"What a spaz," a girl halfway up the line said loudly to her friends. They all laughed, and Ronald glanced toward them with a hurt-puppy-dog expression in his big brown eyes. I couldn't help feeling a little bit sorry for him. After all, he didn't choose to be a doofus. He was just born that way.

The lunch lady sent him to the back of the line to buy another lunch. He looked so totally pathetic as he took his place behind me that I figured it was my duty as a good citizen to do what I could to make him feel better.

"Hi, Ronald," I said, smiling at him as nicely as I could. "Bummer about your lunch."

"Hi, Jessica." He wiped a blob of split-pea soup off his cheek. I noticed a chunk of ham clinging to his hair and wrinkled my nose.

Remembering the extra tissue in my jeans pocket, I dug it out. "Here," I said, handing it to Ronald. "I think you need this a lot more than I do."

"Thanks. Thanks a lot, Jessica." He smiled at me gratefully as he accepted the tissue and attempted to clean the gunk off his hands and clothes. He didn't notice the ham in his hair, and I couldn't bring myself to point it out. So I just tried not to look at it.

The line was moving again, and I turned to follow the guy in front of me, feeling kind of pleased with myself. Certain people, like my twin sister, Elizabeth, for instance, claim that I'm not always very nice to socially challenged people like Ronald. I almost wished she'd been there to witness how incredibly kind and thoughtful I'd just been. Of course, if Elizabeth had been there, I probably wouldn't have had a chance to be nice. She would have rushed off and borrowed a whole roll of paper towels and then picked every piece of revolting ham out of Ronald's hair herself.

I couldn't help but smile at the mental image

of Elizabeth wringing pea soup out of Ronald's button-down shirt.

"I should have known something like that would happen," Ronald commented loudly as he grabbed a tray and stepped up next to me. "It's my shoes."

"Uh, what?" My smile faded a little. I'd practically forgotten he was still standing there.

"My shoes," Ronald repeated. He poked me on the arm to make sure I was paying attention. "I just got them last weekend, and the soles are still really slippery. That's why I fell."

I glanced at his thick-soled brown shoes. Aside from the little puddle of greenish soup on the toe of the left one, they did look pretty shiny and new. "Oh," I responded. I noticed that the guy in front of me was checking us out over his shoulder. The last thing I wanted to do was stand around in public talking to Ronald Rheece about his choice in footwear. That went way beyond a good deed. It was more like social suicide.

Ronald was holding up one foot and pointing at the bottom of his shoe, almost tipping over again a few times as he hopped on the other foot, trying to keep his balance. "See? Totally smooth."

"Hmmm," was all I could muster before I

turned to face the front of the line. I hoped he'd get the hint.

He didn't.

"It's pretty hard for me to find shoes that fit," he announced, carefully setting a new bowl of pea soup on his tray. It smelled like my brother's dirty gym socks. "I have wide toes and a narrow heel."

I gritted my teeth as the line crept forward, wondering how long I had to continue this conversation before I could nominate myself for sainthood. "That's nice, Ronald."

Ronald reached into the pocket of his khakis and pulled out a handful of change. He dumped it on his tray and counted it quickly. "Uh-oh." He looked worried, digging into his pockets again. But his hands came up empty except for a couple of pennies and a set of house keys on a key chain with big red letters I couldn't make out. *It probably says something like I Love Calculus,* I thought. I wasn't about to get close enough to find out. "I spent most of my money on the first lunch. I don't think I have enough left to buy another one. I'm a quarter short."

What a tragedy, I thought, glancing with disgust at the pea soup. That was a mistake. My stomach started to churn.

But Ronald seemed pretty upset. "I don't

know what to do," he exclaimed, searching his pockets yet again. "When I don't eat, I get terrible headaches."

I was starting to feel a headache coming on myself—and it wasn't just from the pea-soup fumes. Out of the corner of my eye I could see that a bunch of the other kids in line were looking at us. If I wasn't careful, everyone would start thinking that Ronald and I were actually friends. And then my reputation would be set— Jessica Wakefield, Nerd Girl.

"Here," I said, digging a dollar out of my pocket and tossing it onto his tray. "It's on me."

I figured that would shut him up. I was wrong.

"Wow! Thanks a million, Jessica," Ronald gushed, snatching up the dollar and staring at it as if it were a fifty-dollar bill. "That's *so* nice of you. I'll pay you back tomorrow, I promise."

"Whatever," I muttered, wishing I could take the money back. We had *finally* reached the juice case, and I snatched a carton and prepared to make a quick escape as soon as I got past the cash register. But Ronald caught up with me just past the register.

"Thanks again for the loan, Jessica," he said, scurrying along to keep up. "I really appreciate it."

I was getting the sinking feeling that he

planned to sit down and have lunch with me. I could almost see the surprised look on Bethel's face when I headed for our usual table with King Geek trailing along behind me like a short, skinny, orthopedic-shoe-wearing shadow. There was no way I was going to let that happen. It was time to take some action.

"Look!" I said suddenly, pointing to the windows at one end of the cafeteria. "Something just happened in the sky."

I happen to know that Ronald is a sucker for anything mathematical or scientific. He takes a special calculus class over at the high school every morning, and he's always talking about computers and radio waves and stuff like that. For the past few days he'd been blabbing about some science lecture he was dying to go to over at Sweet Valley University. Something to do with quarks, I think. It sounded incredibly boring to me.

Ronald spun around immediately, almost spilling his soup again. "Where?" he demanded eagerly.

That was all I needed to make my escape. I darted away quickly, wondering who exactly was in charge of assigning locker partners and when I'd ever have a chance for revenge.

A n n a

It's been almost a year, I thought as I carelessly tossed my books into my locker.

The dread had been building in me for days now, more and more with each passing hour. *It's been almost a year since my brother died.* I shut my eyes, trying to push back all the pain that stung me as those words ran through my head.

It had been hard to deal with the fact that Tim was gone—really, totally, gone forever— every day since the accident. But lately, as the first anniversary of the day that stupid drunk driver killed my brother got closer and closer, it had started feeling pretty much impossible. Sometimes I wasn't sure I was really existing at all. It just seemed like I was in someone's horrible nightmare.

But the really awful part was that I still had to fake being okay. I had to get up and brush my teeth and go to school and take tests and talk to people as if everything were still totally normal. Like earlier today, when Elizabeth had looked at

15

me with that really concerned expression on her face, I'd had to resist the temptation to tell her everything I was feeling. I'd had to remind myself there was no way she could possibly understand. She still had her big brother, along with a twin sister and a nice father and a mother who didn't spend half her time sitting in a room by herself with all the lights off.

I made it through another day without bursting into tears or spilling out my soul, I thought with a twisted sense of pride as I reached out to close my locker.

"Yo, Anna." Salvador loped up to me as the door banged shut. "What are you up to?"

I shrugged. "Nothing," I told him, pushing my hair back to keep it out of my face. I suddenly noticed that Salvador was staring at my left shoulder with a big grin. "What?"

"Is that some new off-the-shoulder style or something?" he asked. "You know I don't usually care about that kind of girlie stuff. But I must say, I like it. It's definitely you."

"Huh?" I looked down. Sure enough, about five inches of skin was visible through the enormous rip in the seam of my T-shirt. I sighed. "Oh. I guess I didn't notice." I stuffed my hands in my jeans pockets, feeling a crumpled piece of paper in the right-hand pocket.

"Whatever." Salvador had already lost interest. He has the attention span of a peanut sometimes. "So how about hitting the Cue Café with me? We could play cards for a while."

For a second I considered it. Salvador and I used to spend a lot of time together. We hadn't done that as much lately, though.

"I don't think so," I told him. "I'm not in the mood."

"Oh, come on." Salvador fluttered his eyelashes at me and pressed his hands together as if he were praying. "Pretty please? I'll let you pick the game. I'll even let you win a few times."

That was definitely a joke since he almost *never* beat me at cards, no matter what game we were playing. Part of the fun of playing with him was always waiting to see what excuses he'd come up with to explain why he lost. My favorite was the time he claimed he'd had an alien-abduction blackout during a game of crazy eights.

But Salvador's clowning around wasn't making me smile the way it usually did.

I can't believe he hasn't even noticed how I'm feeling this week, I thought with a flash of anger. *He's my best friend. He was friends with Tim. He should know, he should remember. . . .*

He didn't seem to realize that I was staring at

him. He was too busy trying to change my mind. "Please, Anna?" he pleaded. "Come with me. You wouldn't want me to shrivel up and die of loneliness, would you? Just imagine the guilt."

Why was he so eager to hang out with me that afternoon? *Maybe he really misses me.* My annoyance started to fade. *Maybe Salvador is as bummed as I am that we haven't hung out together as much lately.*

No, I remembered, my heart dropping. *It's because Elizabeth won't be around. She's going straight home to do her homework after school. She told us at lunch.*

Now I was even more certain that I didn't want to go to the Cue Café with Salvador. If there was one thing I really couldn't deal with today, it was wondering what the deal was between him and Elizabeth. They claimed they were just friends now, and for a little while it had seemed like maybe Salvador was interested in me. But he'd been sending out some pretty confusing signals, and I wasn't sure if he liked either of us anymore.

Of course, I wasn't wasting a whole lot of time thinking about any of that these days. I had other things on my mind. Things that Salvador, apparently, had totally forgotten about.

Maybe we'll never be the kind of best friends we

used to be, I thought miserably. *Just one more stupid, horrible thing about growing up.*

"Well?" Salvador was leaning against the next locker, looking at me expectantly. "So are we going or what?"

"Or what," I replied, slinging my backpack over my shoulder. "You'll just have to entertain yourself for a change. You've always been really good at that anyway."

I hurried away before he could answer.

Salvador

"He shoots, he scores!" I announced, spinning around and winging my Kit Kat wrapper at the big metal wastebasket at the corner of Third and Sunset. I'd found the half-eaten candy bar in the bottom of my backpack when I'd put my books in there at the end of the day. It was slightly smushed and a little stale, but otherwise it had really hit the spot.

The wrapper bounced off the rim and landed inside the trash can. I glanced around automatically for someone to admire my awesome shot. But nobody was there except an old guy sweeping the sidewalk in front of Sunset Liquors. And he didn't even glance my way.

"Nice shot, Salvador," I told myself loudly, reaching around to pat myself on the shoulder. "You're a basketball god."

The old guy finally looked up and sort of scowled. That made me smile for a second. But only a second. Somehow that kind of stuff is always a lot funnier if there's someone else around to see it.

"That really was an awesome shot, Salvador," I told myself in a falsetto voice. "Thanks, Anna," I said in my normal voice. "You're too kind. So should we go play some cards?" I switched back to the falsetto to respond, "Of course, Salvador. You know I'm always happy to hang out with my best friend in the whole world."

I sighed. What was Anna's problem anyway? Since when was she all weird about spending time with me? Usually if she had something else to do, like a doctor's appointment or something, she would just say so.

I hope she hasn't figured out what happened at the party, I thought, feeling a cold shiver go down my spine. *She was pretty upset that time when Elizabeth and I went out without her. I can't even imagine what she'd think if she knew that we actually kissed. . . .*

That brought my mind back to its almost constant preoccupation: The Kiss. I'd even started thinking about it in capital letters. It was that major.

I wondered if Elizabeth still thought about it too. It was hard to tell since she never mentioned it. Maybe it hadn't meant as much to her as it had to me. Or maybe it had. Basically I had no idea.

21

"Just call me Salvador del Valle, the Great Clueless One," I muttered.

Sighing loudly and swinging my backpack as I walked, I wished for the twelve-millionth time that I knew what to do about The Elizabeth Wakefield Situation. I'd started thinking about *that* in capital letters too. Lately everything I couldn't make sense of ended up in caps in my head—which made for a pretty crowded brain. The only thing I knew for sure was that I wanted to kiss Elizabeth again. And again. And then kiss her some more.

But that was where the simple part stopped. I'd spent hours trying to figure out if Elizabeth felt the same way, and it just gave me a headache.

And then there was Anna. She was my best friend, and I hated upsetting her. For some reason, she seemed to freak at the whole idea of me and Elizabeth together. She'd never really said so or anything, but Anna wasn't exactly the queen of subtlety when she was upset.

It's like she feels left out or something, I thought. *Like she's afraid we're going to ditch her and leave her all alone.*

I kicked at a loose stone on the sidewalk. It hit a crack and flew up to one side, almost hitting the plate-glass window of Susie Q's Card

Shoppe. I heaved a sigh of relief as it bounced off the bricks below the window instead. I could only imagine what the Doña, my grandmother, would say if she got a window-repair bill from Susie Q in the mail. She's pretty cool as grandmothers go, but she does have limits.

There was a woman setting up a Halloween display inside the card-shop window. I guess she heard the stone bounce off the wall because she shot me a dirty look. I wondered if she was Susie Q. I also wondered if she realized that Halloween was still ten days away. I guessed not since she was busy setting up a bunch of Halloween cards on top of a gigantic papier-mâché pumpkin. As I paused to watch, she carefully balanced a card shaped like a bat right on top of the fake pumpkin's stem.

That made me think of Anna again. She's got this weird thing about bats. She thinks they're the cutest creatures on earth. Never mind the blood-sucking vampire thing or the fact that they look like grungy little rats with wings. For some reason, she thinks they're adorable.

"Salvador! Yo, Salvador, hold up!"

I turned away from the window to see who was calling me. It was Brian Rainey. He raced along the sidewalk, his long blond hair flying in all directions. A second later he skidded to a halt in front of me.

"Hey, I'm glad I caught you," he said breathlessly, pushing his hair back into place. "I need your help."

"What's up?" I said. Brian's a good guy. He mostly hangs with the cool crowd at school, so I wouldn't say we're really close friends or anything. But I'd gotten to know him a little better since he volunteered to help with *Zone*. Besides, he's the kind of guy everybody just automatically likes—guys, girls, teachers, whoever. If I didn't like him so much myself, I'd probably be jealous.

"I'm supposed to go check out the Sweet Valley Tower with Elizabeth after dinner." Brian looked worried as he glanced at his watch. "But I just remembered that my little sister's school play is tonight." He spread out his hands helplessly. "There's no way I can miss that. Can you help me out?"

"Sure thing!" I could hardly believe my awesome luck. This could be my shot. My big chance to find out once and for all if there was any chance Elizabeth liked me as more than a friend. Ever since the party it had been almost impossible to get her alone, away from Anna and everybody else. But tonight she would be trapped high atop the Sweet Valley Tower, all alone with me. The thought made my palms start to sweat. I smiled as calmly as I could. "I happen to be free tonight," I told him casually. "Count me in."

"Cool." Brian looked relieved. He checked his watch again. "Listen, I've got to book. I probably won't have time to call Elizabeth and let her know about the change in plans, so—"

"No problem," I interrupted. "Don't worry about it. What time were you going to meet her there?"

"I was going to have my dad drive us both over. I was supposed to pick her up around seven."

This was too good.

"Got it," I said. "I'm sure the Doña can drive us."

"Thanks, man. I owe you one. I'll call you when I get home tonight to see how it went, okay?" With a wave, Brian jogged on past me and disappeared around the corner.

I turned to head for home, hoping that the Doña didn't have one of her classes tonight. If she did, I'd just have to convince her to blow it off so she could drive me and Elizabeth to the Tower. There was no way I was going to miss this opportunity: Elizabeth Wakefield by moonlight.

I felt a million times better than I had just a few minutes earlier. Well, half a million anyway. But then I remembered Anna. I was pretty sure she wouldn't be very happy when she found out about my little trip to the Tower with Elizabeth. . . .

Suddenly I glanced back over my shoulder at Susie Q's Card Shoppe, and I had a flash of inspiration. I could buy her a goofy bat-shaped card, write some nice little message, and then drop it in her mailbox on my way past her house. That should cheer her up.

I turned and strode toward Susie Q's, feeling pretty proud of myself. Just a few minutes ago I'd been totally lost, and now it looked like all my problems would soon be solved.

Bat Card from Salvador to Anna

Dear Anna,
   So my new bat buddy and I were
wondering if you're okay. We really
hope so because you're our best
friend well, okay, maybe just mine.
The bat says he prefers Dracula,
but you shouldn't take it person-
ally. He has no taste.
   But anyway, you're definitely my
best friend. So if you need to talk
or anything, just let me know and
I'll fly on over anytime you want
me to. That's what I'm here for,
right?
                    Love, Salvador

Jessica

"Hi, Jessica!" a loud, eager voice greeted me as I came out of the gym after track practice that afternoon.

I winced. There was no mistaking that high-pitched, slightly nasal voice.

"Hi, Ronald," I said. "Um, did you just get out of a Future Scientists of America meeting or something?"

"No," he answered. "I was waiting for you."

I glanced around quickly, wondering if anyone had heard him. Luckily most of my track teammates were still inside. There were a couple of ninth-graders hanging out on the sidewalk, but I was pretty sure they were too far away to hear. "You were?" I asked Ronald cautiously. "Uh, why?"

"I just wanted to pay back that dollar you loaned me." He held out a crisp dollar bill. "Thanks again."

I had almost forgotten about that stupid loan, especially since I hadn't even seen Ronald since lunch.

"You're welcome," I said quickly, grabbing the dollar and then scanning the street for my older brother, Steven, who was supposed to pick me up after practice. He was late as usual.

"So, where are you off to now, Jessica?" Ronald gazed at me with a geeky little smile. "Are you going home? Or are you going out for a snack or something? Maybe meeting up with your, uh, sister?"

My heart sank. *Uh-oh,* I thought. *I think I see what's going on here.* As I took in Ronald's eager expression, the way he'd waited for me to get out of practice, I knew there was no other explanation. My noble gesture at lunch had led to something terrible—Ronald had a crush on me!

There was no way I would ever go out with a dorky, science-obsessed guy like Ronald Rheece. Not even if an asteroid wiped out the entire rest of the planet and the future of the human race depended on it. But I couldn't just ignore him—I mean, I didn't want to hurt his feelings or anything.

"Nope, I'm just going home," I said briskly. "My brother will be here any second. So don't let me keep you or anything. I'm sure you have places to be, things to do. You know, um, ham radios to work on or whatever."

"Not really." Ronald shrugged, still smiling

29

that goofy smile. "I don't mind hanging out while you wait."

"Um, okay." I wasn't sure what else to say that wouldn't be totally mean and obnoxious, like, *You may not mind, but I do,* or just, *Get lost, loser.* Suddenly I had an idea. "You might not want to stand too close, though," I said. "I just finished track practice, and I'm all sweaty and stinky. Pretty gross, huh?" I glanced at him hopefully. Actually, I had taken a shower before changing back into my regular clothes. But I figured Ronald might not be able to tell.

Once again my brilliant plan backfired. Ronald actually took a step closer and *sniffed.* "You don't stink at all," he said. "You smell really nice. Like flowers or something."

Curse that honeysuckle shampoo I'd borrowed from Elizabeth! Maybe it was the karma of the universe punishing me since I never exactly told her that I was borrowing it. "Thanks," I muttered. "It's just my sister's shampoo."

I was getting pretty desperate by now. I knew that if Steven pulled up and saw me talking to a nerdy guy like Ronald, he'd never let me hear the end of it. He'd probably start calling me Mrs. Jessica W. Dorkenstein or something. He doesn't have the most sophisticated sense of humor in the world.

But I'd had thirteen years' experience ignoring Steven's obnoxious comments. I was a lot more worried about what my track teammates would think if they came out and saw us here. Especially if Ronald started batting his eyes or trying to put his arm around me in front of them.

"Is it jasmine?" he asked.

I was so busy thinking about the highly possible death of my entire social life that I guess I'd kind of zoned out on what Ronald was saying. I blinked at him, startled. "What?"

"That smell," he said patiently. "Elizabeth's shampoo. It's so pretty and flowery. She has great taste. What is it? Roses?" He leaned a little closer and took another big whiff.

I backed away, almost ready to give up on my polite approach. I mean, what kind of guy goes right up to a girl and starts smelling her? Even a nerd like Ronald should know better than that.

"So is it roses?" he repeated.

I thought fast. "Um, no, actually, you caught me, Ronald," I said, trying to look embarrassed. That wasn't too hard—all I had to do was imagine what Bethel and Mary and the others would think if they happened to walk out of the gym right about now. "It's not shampoo at all. It's medicine. I just rubbed it all over this huge rash

I have on my back." I shrugged and laughed. "I'm not sure where it came from, but it's getting bigger all the time. And sort of oozing."

I knew I was taking a risk by saying something like that. I could only imagine what would happen if word got out around school that I was, like, some kind of leper or something. Still, it wasn't as though Ronald ever talked to anybody cool.

Ronald looked worried. "That sounds kind of serious."

"Uh-huh," I said quickly. "I mean, it's *probably* not anything contagious. But you never know."

"Have you been to the doctor?"

"Um, no." I had just spotted Mom's car turning the corner at the end of the block with Steven at the wheel. "I'm sure it'll go away soon. Look, there's my ride. See you."

I rushed toward the car without waiting for Ronald to respond. I slammed the door and collapsed in the seat with a huge sigh of relief. I'd *finally* escaped.

"What's with you?" Steven gave me a curious look. He glanced out the window, where Ronald was probably still standing on the sidewalk. I was being very careful not to look that way. "Who's that you were talking to?"

"Nobody," I said quickly. "Just someone asking for directions."

Steven snorted. "From you?" he said as he put the car into gear. "Poor guy. He'll never get any-where."

I ignored my brother's lame attempt at humor. "You can say that again," I muttered under my breath as we drove away.

A n n a

I trudged up the steps to my porch, and stopped at the front door. I reached out to grab the door handle, and I just stood there, twisting the knob around without even getting the key out of my backpack.

Then I let go, turning around to stare at all the other houses on my block. I saw a little girl and her mom walking through their door, hand in hand.

I took a deep breath, sitting down on our porch swing and dropping my bag down next to me. I started to swing slowly, enjoying the easy rhythm of the motion and the loud creaks as it moved back and forth, back and forth.

It must be nice not to dread going into your own house, I thought, stuffing my hands into my pockets and letting my feet graze the porch floor. My fingertips touched something— the old piece of paper I'd felt in my pocket earlier.

Curious, I pulled it out, smoothing out the creases so I could read it.

I remember kindergarten:
You ate my paste.

I sucked in my breath. It was the poem I'd never given to Salvador. It must have been in my jeans ever since the Wakefields' party. I shuddered, remembering how badly that night had ended.

What would have happened if Salvador had seen this? I wondered, sitting up straighter as the swing came to a stop. I blushed, an image popping into my head from the daydream I'd been having pretty frequently about the two of us together. . . .

I shook my head. How could I even *think* about that right now? I glanced back down at the poem and began to tear it up. Salvador, my supposed best friend, couldn't even remember what this week was. He couldn't even figure out that something was bothering me! How could I even think about going out with him when he hardly seemed to notice me at all?

Hot tears burned my eyes as I finished shredding the poem. *Salvador's the one who was supposed to understand,* I told myself, blinking furiously. Was I the only one who cared that Tim was gone forever and that this was when it happened?

"Anna?"

My head shot up, and I saw my mom standing over me in her bathrobe, her expression as blank as ever.

"Hi, Mom," I said dully, jumping up and wiping my hand quickly across my eyes.

"What are you doing out here?" she asked, glancing vaguely around.

"Just, you know, enjoying the nice breeze," I said. It was a totally windless day.

She nodded. "Okay, sweetie, I'm going back inside. Are you coming?"

I bit my lip, staring down at the porch.

"Yeah, uh-huh," I mumbled, waiting as she unlocked the door.

I paused for a second before following her, wondering if she would turn around. *Come on, Mom,* I pleaded inwardly. *Let me know that you're feeling all of this too, that you remember!*

I watched her as she moved slowly through the living room. I kept staring until her back disappeared around the corner.

My heart sank. I sighed, stepping inside and shutting the front door behind me.

Elizabeth

When the doorbell rang at seven o'clock, I jumped up from the kitchen table, where I was putting the finishing touches on my algebra homework. "I'll get it," I told my parents, who were at the other end of the table, having some tea.

I hurried through the living room. Jessica and Steven were sprawled at opposite ends of the couch in front of the TV, arguing about which of them should get up and answer the door.

"Never mind," I told them both. "It's for me."

Jessica's eyes lit up. "Oh, right," she said. "You're going out with Brian Rainey tonight. Lucky you." She smirked and winked.

"Little Lizzie has a date?" Steven raised one eyebrow. "On a weeknight? Well, don't do anything I wouldn't do."

"Very funny," I said. "You know perfectly well it's not a date. We're doing research for an article."

"Whatever." Jessica rolled her eyes. Steven

just grinned and made a few obnoxious kissing noises before returning his attention to the television.

I ignored them both and swung open the door. "Hi, Brian," I said.

I froze and did a double take when I realized it wasn't Brian standing there on the doorstep. It was Salvador.

"Surprise," he sang out with a grin.

"What are you doing here?"

"Escorting you to the tallest, most magnificent tower in at least a three-mile radius." Salvador waved his arm at a car idling at the curb. "Our chariot awaits."

For some reason, his silly sense of humor didn't amuse me nearly as much as it usually did. "What do you mean?" I said, confused. "Where's Brian?"

Salvador shrugged. "He couldn't make it. He had to go to his little sister's play."

My body tensed up at the idea of going to a superromantic spot with Salvador, the guy I was struggling to avoid thinking about in the same sentence as the word *romantic*. And I was frustratingly aware of the way the porch light made his hair, which was usually almost black, glow a rich, deep brown. I took a deep breath.

What do I do now? I asked myself frantically.

Why didn't Brian call me if he couldn't make it? Then I could have rescheduled or at least called Anna to come along with us. . . .

Just then Jessica appeared at the door beside me, her most flirtatious smile pasted on her face. "Hi," she purred throatily. But as soon as she saw Salvador, she frowned. "Oh," she said in her regular voice. "It's just El Salvador."

"Nice slippers, Jessica," Salvador said, straight-faced. "Where'd you get them—did a sheep explode?"

He laughed at his own joke as Jessica rolled her eyes and wandered back toward the couch. I was feeling too annoyed at Salvador's surprise appearance to laugh, even though Jessica's fuzzy white slippers really did look like shrapnel from some barnyard disaster. Actually, for some strange reason, the fact that Salvador had said something I thought was funny annoyed me even more.

"Well, come on, then," I said flatly, grabbing my notebook off the hall table. "If we're going, let's go."

Salvador shot me a puzzled look, but he shrugged and stepped aside to let me pass. "After you."

I marched toward his grandmother's car without a backward glance. "Hello, Elizabeth," the

Doña said, smiling at me as I opened the back door of her car and climbed inside. "How are you?"

"I'm fine, thank you," I replied politely, forcing myself to smile. "Thanks for driving us, Mrs. del Valle."

Salvador hurried around to the other side of the car and opened the other back door. "What are you doing?" I asked as he slid onto the backseat beside me.

He glanced at his legs, then at the car seat. "Well, I'm not sure," he said, scratching his head and pretending to look mystified. "But I think it's calling 'getting into the car.'"

"No," I said, trying to keep my patience. Why was everything he did and said rubbing me the wrong way tonight? "I mean, aren't you going to sit up front with your grandmother?"

Salvador pulled his door shut. "I can sit with her anytime. I'd rather sit with you."

"It's all right, Elizabeth," the Doña said, turning to glance at me. "I don't mind playing chauffeur. Besides, Salvador always turns the radio up too loud when he sits in the front seat."

"But . . ." I bit my lip and glanced forward. The Doña was already turning the key in the ignition. What could I say? *Sorry, Salvador, I really don't want to sit next to you right now because even though you're one of my best friends, being in a confined space with you is really freaking me out?* Somehow I didn't think that would help the situation much.

We pulled away from the curb and headed down my street. I knew we were only riding across town to the Sweet Valley Tower. But right then it felt more like we were setting off on a cross-country trek to the Empire State Building.

"So," Salvador said after a few seconds of silence. "What's our angle on this article anyway? Moonlight, did you say?"

"That's the plan," I replied shortly.

"Good plan," he said. "Moonlight rules."

I wasn't sure what that was supposed to mean, so I just shrugged. "I guess."

He fell silent again after that, and I slumped into the corner of the backseat, staring at the back of Salvador's grandmother's head and feeling guilty and confused. *What's wrong with me anyway?* I wondered. *Why am I acting like this?*

All Alone
by Anna Wang

I turn to you
but your chair is empty.
I save the last bite
but your plate is missing.

I see your friends,
still together.
Talking, laughing,
still living.

We were ripped apart,
and now you're gone.
But I'm still here,
all alone.

Salvador

Why is she being so cold? I asked myself, sneaking a quick peek at Elizabeth. *If I didn't know better, I'd think I'd gotten into the car with the wrong Wakefield twin. The* evil *one.* She was sort of huddled against the car door as if she wanted it to open and dump her out on the pavement.

Of course, I wasn't helping things much myself. It wasn't until the joke about Jessica's bedroom slippers was out of my mouth that I realized it might not be exactly the thing to get the evening off to a smooth start. I mean, Elizabeth has a great sense of humor and everything. But maybe making fun of her identical twin sister was pushing things a little too far.

Then there had been that idiotic comment about moonlight. *Moonlight rules?* Where had my mouth come up with that one? My brain certainly had no idea.

Still, the silence in the backseat was really getting to me. The only sound inside the whole car was the Doña humming along with the radio, which was playing a funky reggae song.

I turned to Elizabeth and jerked my thumb toward my grandmother. "Check it out, mon," I said. "The Doña's probably the only grandmother in the state who can groove to Bob Marley. Having such a musical genius in the family can be a drag sometimes, though, like when she was taking that Introduction to Bagpiping class last year."

The Doña smiled at me in the rearview mirror, then turned up the radio a little and kept humming.

"I like bagpipe music," Elizabeth said, keeping her eyes focused forward. She hadn't looked at me since we'd started driving.

"You wouldn't if it woke you up at six A.M. every Saturday morning," I joked weakly. It was getting harder and harder for me to act like my normal charming self. I mean, Elizabeth certainly wasn't acting like *her*self. She's usually really nice and easy to talk to. I actually found myself wondering if it was some kind of weird werewolf-type thing—you know, like whenever the moon is full, she gets possessed and switches personalities. It was possible. I mean, I guess I hadn't known her *all* that long.

The Doña put on her turn signal as she

reached the intersection of Rush Avenue and Tower Street. "Almost there, kids," she said. "I've got to do some shopping, so I'll just swing back and pick you up when I'm finished, all right? I shouldn't be more than an hour."

Glancing out the window, I saw the Sweet Valley Tower just ahead of us. At least this horrible car ride was almost over. Maybe Elizabeth just felt weird talking to me in front of the Doña. Maybe things would get more normal once we got to the top of the tower. At least I hoped so.

To: WakefieldSV
From: RadioRon
Re: Greetings and salutations
Message:

Hi, Jessica! It's Ronald Rheece. I hope you don't mind that I looked up your family's e-mail address. It's amazing how easy it is to access the school's computer records if you know what you're doing. They really should do something about their online security, or they could start to have problems with hackers.

Anyway, I've been worrying about your you-know-what that you told me about you-know-when. I have an idea about what you could do for it. I'll try to call you later and talk to you about it.

By the way, do you happen to know anyone who might be interested in that science lecture I was telling you about? I would ask you, but I know you're not very interested in science. But anyway, I really wish I didn't have to go to the lecture alone. Those sorts of things are always more fun if you have someone intelligent to discuss it with afterward.

By the way, in case the rest of the family is reading this too, hello!

Elizabeth

The elevator ride to the top of the
Sweet Valley Tower seemed to last forever. The
only other person in there with us was an old
woman with blue-tinted white hair and a camera. She kept glancing at us suspiciously, as if
she thought we might try to steal her camera or
something. It might have been kind of funny if
I'd been in the mood to laugh. But Salvador
barely seemed to notice the old woman. He was
too busy staring at *me*. And I was too busy
avoiding his stare. So the three of us made the
long ride up to the observation deck in total
silence.

Finally we reached the top. The elevator
doors opened onto a little square lobby encased
in thick glass, with a set of double doors lead-
ing to the open observation deck that ran all
around the top part of the tower. On the table
to one side of the elevator, I spotted a stack of
leaflets giving the history of the tower and
snagged one, figuring it could come in handy

for the article. Meanwhile Salvador hurried to the glass doors and pulled one open, holding it for the old woman. She stepped through it with a few words of thanks, and then Salvador turned to me. "After you," he said, still holding the door open.

Salvador isn't usually the gentlemanly type. Flustered, I hurried through the door, avoiding his gaze. As I stepped onto the observation deck, a cool breeze wafted past, lifting my hair slightly off my face. I took a deep breath, feeling some of my tension melt away.

I turned to a clean page in my notebook and walked toward the railing. It had been years since I'd been up here, and I'd almost forgotten what the tower was like. When I was little, I used to think the Sweet Valley Tower was the highest place in the entire world. Now I know better, but when I glanced up and saw the stars twinkling in the clear sky that seemed only a short distance above me, I still felt like I was on top of the world instead of just a few hundred feet above Sweet Valley.

Glancing over my shoulder, I saw that Salvador was still standing just outside the glass doors. He was gazing around, taking in the viewing scopes placed every few yards along the metal railing; the wide, almost empty observation deck; and the security guard dozing in a folding chair near the glass doors. I expected him to start cracking jokes and making fun of it all.

But instead he just shrugged. "This is nice," he said.

The blue-haired old woman had gone straight to the railing a few yards down from where I was standing and started snapping pictures. By the time Salvador had finished taking his first look around and joined me at the railing, she had finished her photographing and replaced the lens cap on her camera. As she passed us, heading back toward the elevator enclosure, she nodded at us. "Have a nice evening, kids," she said in a quavery voice.

"Thanks," I said.

Salvador smiled at her. "You have a nice night too."

Soon the old woman disappeared into the elevator lobby, and Salvador and I had the observation deck to ourselves. Well, except for the guard, that is, who was still snoozing away in his chair. *Sleeping people don't exactly count,* I told myself. So really, the two of us were . . . alone.

Alone, sort of the way we'd been in Steven's

room that night at the party. The night Salvador and I had kissed.

"So what do you think?" I asked, hoping that the moon wouldn't provide enough light for Salvador to see the rosy patches of color I felt spreading across my cheeks. "Quite a view, huh?"

"Yeah." Salvador leaned on the railing and gazed out over the town.

For a few long minutes we just stood side by side and checked out the view. The sun had set, and the streetlights were twinkling in the grid of streets below. Farther out, as the roads and neighborhoods followed the shape of the hills and canyons, the lights were spread out more. We were facing west, and if I squinted, I could make out the blue shimmer of the Pacific Ocean on the horizon, stretching away into infinity.

I was the first one to break the silence.

"It's so peaceful up here," I murmured, leaning on the railing and gazing down at the town again. "It's almost magical."

Salvador nodded. When he spoke, his voice was quieter than usual. "You're right," he agreed. He cleared his throat. "You know, I've never actually been up here before."

"Really?" I was a little surprised. "It's pretty

cool to see all the places that are so familiar at ground level from up here. They look different somehow." I leaned over a little farther and pointed to a two-story, brown-brick building off to the right of the tower. "See? There's our school."

"Hey!" Salvador grinned when he saw it. "You're right. It does look different." He peered a little farther over in the same direction. "Check it out—there's my house. And the mall."

I spent the next few minutes pointing out different places around Sweet Valley. We spotted all the places where we like to hang out after school, like the Cue Café and Vito's Pizza, as well as other landmarks like the hospital and the town hall.

Finally Salvador laughed. "Wow," he said. "You know where everything is, don't you? You must have been here a lot."

"My family came here a bunch of times when I was little, but we haven't been up here in years." I smiled. "I really used to love it."

Salvador turned to me with a serious expression.

"What were you like when you were little?" he asked, staring right into my eyes.

I glanced away, at the mountains far off in the east. "Well," I said, wondering how to answer. It was kind of a weird question, especially from someone like him. "I guess I was sort of the same way I am now. I mean, I've always liked the same kinds of things—reading, writing, hanging out with my friends."

When I looked back at Salvador, he was still gazing back at me intently. He didn't say anything, but I could tell he was listening. *Really* listening.

I could feel my face getting hot as I babbled on. But Salvador looked interested, so I kept talking. "I remember the last time I was here," I said, "It was on Jessica's and my birthday. I think we were turning eight, or maybe nine. We wore matching dresses." I smiled at the memory. "Jessica picked them out—she said it was because they matched our eyes. Even then she was into fashion."

Salvador laughed. But his laugh sounded different than it usually did—softer and more subdued. "You two must have looked really cute like that," he said. "Wearing matching outfits, I mean."

I shrugged. "We used to dress alike a lot when we were little," I said. "Anyway, it was my idea to come up here that day. Jessica didn't want to—she never liked this tower much." I rolled my eyes. "She said it was boring to stare

52

down at stuff instead of going down and seeing it up close."

The guard let out a loud snore and shifted in his chair. Salvador and I glanced over at him, then at each other. Without a word, we both started to giggle.

"I've got the perfect title for our article," Salvador said between gasps of laughter. "'Sweet Valley Tower by Moonlight: What a Snore!'"

That made me laugh even harder. I clapped a hand over my mouth to stifle the sound, not wanting to wake up the guard. I shouldn't have worried. At that moment he shifted again with a loud snort and a sigh.

Salvador and I really lost it then. I was having serious trouble breathing. He was just as bad. His shoulders shook up and down, and he leaned on the railing weakly, laughing hysterically.

When we had managed to regain our composure, Salvador looked over at me. "Sorry," he said. "You were saying?"

Another giggle popped out of my mouth, and then I continued my story. "I finally talked Jessica into coming here on our birthday," I said, resting my elbows on the railing. My stomach hurt a little from laughing so hard. "At first she just stomped around acting bored. But finally she came over and stood next to me. I was looking for our house."

Salvador leaned a little farther over the railing, suddenly looking curious. "Where is it?"

"You can't see it from here." I shook my head and smiled. "Jessica and I searched for ages that day before we realized it's hidden." I pointed in the direction of my neighborhood. "See? It's in the little valley behind that hill."

"Too bad," Salvador commented.

"That's what Jessica said too." I brushed back a strand of hair as the breeze tossed it across my face. "But then she had a great idea. It was just starting to get dark by that time, and she looked up and spotted the first star."

"Star light, star bright, first star I see tonight," Salvador quoted, glancing up at the hundreds of stars scattered across the dark sky before returning his attention to me. "Did you make a wish?"

I nodded. "Jessica told me that since we were so much closer to the sky than usual, we should be sure to make a really *important* wish," I explained. "She also said that because we were twins and it was our birthday, our wish would be twice as likely to come true if we wished it together."

"That's cute." Salvador smiled. "So what did you wish for?"

I hesitated, remembering that evening so long ago. Jessica and I had grasped each other's hands tightly and looked right up at the star. *Star light, star bright,* we had chanted, whispering the entire rhyme. Then we had made our wish silently, looking at each other and knowing we were both thinking the same thing.

"I probably shouldn't tell you," I told Salvador at last. "You're not supposed to say a wish out loud or it won't come true."

"Oh, come on," he pleaded. "I'll never tell—I promise."

I smiled back at him. "Well, all right," I said. "We wished that we would be best friends forever."

I shot him a slightly wary look, waiting for him to make fun of what I'd said. But he just nodded thoughtfully. "I sometimes wish I had a brother or sister," he said softly.

"Really?" I shivered slightly as the breeze tickled my bare arms.

"Are you cold?" Salvador asked quickly.

I shrugged and rubbed my arms with my hands. "Just a little. I should have remembered to bring a sweater."

"Here." Before I could stop him, Salvador had shrugged off the jean jacket he was wearing over his T-shirt. He draped it around my shoulders, carefully brushing my hair out of the way so it wouldn't get caught. "How's that?"

He was standing so close—I could barely breathe. The spot where his fingers had brushed against my neck as he'd lifted my hair was warm and tingly.

He stared at me, his black eyes strangely intense. I knew I should probably say or do something. But I couldn't seem to move. All I could do was gaze back at him as his face moved closer and closer....

And then he kissed me. And every fear and doubt I had was silenced by my excitement.

"Salvador?" the Doña's voice called from over by the elevator.

Salvador broke away immediately. "Uh-oh," he said, stepping back.

I leaned against the railing and gulped, trying to get control of myself.

"Just a minute!" he called back to his grandmother.

"Uh, I guess we've been up here a long time," I stammered, praying that the Doña hadn't seen what we were doing.

No such luck. As she hurried toward us, she had a huge smile on her face. My heart sank. She had seen us—no doubt about it. "Come on, kids," she said. "We've got to get back downstairs before I get a parking ticket."

Salvador and I followed her back to the elevator, avoiding each other's eyes. My mind was racing. *What's wrong with me? Why didn't I stop him? It was lucky the Doña interrupted when she did. Salvador should never have kissed me.*

But I couldn't stop wondering when we'd get a chance to kiss again.

Dear Salvador,

Thanks for the card. The bat was really cute.

I feel like an idiot. I was so sure you hadn't noticed how bummed I've been lately. I thought you'd totally forgotten about Tim. Then I check my mailbox and I find this. . . .

There's just one thing I'm kind of wondering about, though. When you said we'd always be best friends, what did you mean by that exactly? I mean, a while ago I sort of thought maybe you wanted us to be something _more_ than best friends. But then I wasn't so sure.

Anyway, either way I'm glad you gave me the card. Because I could really use a best friend right about now, and you're the best of the best. Unless, you know, you want to be a different kind of . . .

Oh, who am I kidding? It's not like you're ever going to read this. As soon as Mom finishes her bath, I'm going to rip this stupid note to shreds and flush it down the toilet so no one will ever know what a freak I am.

Your best friend (or something),
Anna

Jessica

I sat at the kitchen table, kicking at the leg of my chair. "When do you think Elizabeth will be home?" I asked. "I'm bored."

Mom looked up from her seat across the table, where she was busy paying bills, and rolled her eyes. "As I told you the first thirty-four times you asked, Jessica, I don't know exactly when she'll be home, but I'm sure it will be soon." She ripped the top check out of her checkbook and stuck it in an envelope. "Now, why don't you stop moping around and do something useful, like your homework?"

"I'm not *that* bored," I muttered.

I sighed and leaned my elbows on the table as Mom left the room in search of stamps. Glancing at the digital clock on the microwave oven, I saw that it was almost eight o'clock.

This is totally pathetic, I told myself. *Here I am, sitting around waiting for Elizabeth to get home so I'll have someone to talk to. How sad is that?*

Jessica

I still had plenty of friends—even if my social life wasn't exactly what it used to be. I would just call one of them and see what was going on. I didn't have to sit around here all night, twiddling my thumbs like a loser and waiting for Elizabeth to get home from hanging out with goofy old El Salvador.

I walked to the phone on the wall near the refrigerator, debating what number to dial.

I knew who I *wanted* to call. I sighed again, picturing Damon Ross's adorable eyes and imagining how his voice would sound on the phone. A shiver passed through me at the idea of really calling him.

But there was no way I could do that. I mean, we'd barely ever spoken to each other.

I'll just call Kristin, I decided rationally. Kristin Seltzer was exactly the kind of upbeat, fun person to boost my mood.

I grabbed the receiver and punched in her number, waiting as it rang a couple of times.

"Hello?" a chipper voice answered.

I smiled, leaning against the wall. "Hey, Kristin, it's Jessica."

"Oh, hi, Jess," she responded brightly.

"Guess who I was about to call," I said, twisting the phone cord around my finger.

"Who?" Kristin asked.

"I wouldn't have done it anyway," I said hurriedly. "I mean, I shouldn't, right?"

Kristin sighed. "Jess, I don't know what you're talking about."

"Damon," I interrupted impatiently. "I wanted to call Damon."

"Then why didn't you?"

"So you think I should, then?" I asked eagerly, untangling the knots in the phone cord.

Kristin laughed. "He's a friendly guy—I'm sure he'd be happy to talk," she said.

I rolled my eyes. Kristin was great, but sometimes she was *too* nice.

I heard a click.

"Oh, hang on, Kristin. That's my other line."

"I've gotta go anyway," she replied. "I have a test tomorrow."

"Oh, okay. Talk to you later."

"Bye, Jess."

I pushed down the flash button quickly, then let go.

"Hello?" I said. My heart started to beat faster as I let myself imagine that it was Damon, calling because he couldn't stand to let another minute go by without—

"Good evening," a formal voice said. "Might I speak with Jessica Wakefield, please?"

I sucked in my breath. "Ronald?" I said carefully. "Is that you?"

"You recognized my voice!" He sounded surprised.

I sighed. "Of course I did, Ronald. I hear it every day at our locker," I reminded him. "So why are you calling?" *Please, let him just be selling tickets to the science fair or something,* I hoped.

"Well, I was thinking about what you said today," he said. "You know, about your rash?"

"Um, yes?" My mother had just reentered the room. She glanced over at me and mouthed something about not tying up the line all night.

She returned to her checkbook, and I racked my brain to come up with a way to get Ronald off the phone before he proposed or something.

"You ran off so fast that I didn't get a chance to tell you," he said eagerly. "But my uncle is a skin doctor, and I really think he could help you."

"Oh, really?" I said, trying to keep my tone neutral. Mom was still bent over her envelopes and stuff. "Um, thanks, but that's okay. I think it's getting much better."

"Are you sure?" Ronald insisted. "Better safe

than sorry, you know. Maybe I could just tell him about it and see if he thinks you need to come in and see him. I could even come over to your house and take a look if you want. What color did you say it was again?"

"Um . . ." I couldn't remember if I'd said or not. All I wanted was to put an end to this conversation and hang up. "Uh, purple? But listen, Ronald, I was sort of in the middle of something. . . ."

Mom looked up right away, and I cringed, wishing I hadn't used Ronald's name. Ronald's dad and my dad are both lawyers, and they've known each other for, like, a million years. Mom and Dad are always getting on my case for calling Ronald a nerd, even though I keep explaining that it's just an accurate way of describing him. I mean, when you think about it, saying *Ronald Rheece is a nerd* is really no different than saying *Ned Wakefield is a lawyer* or *Jessica Wakefield is blond*. Now that Mom knew I was talking to Ronald, I would have to be superpolite or I'd end up spending the rest of the night listening to another endless lecture on how I shouldn't stereotype people and judge them by appearances and stuff like that.

"And exactly where did you say it was?"

"What?" I had sort of lost track of the conversation.

"The rash," Ronald reminded me. "Where is it?"

I glanced at Mom again. Her eyes were on her checkbook, but I was sure she was still listening. "Um, you know," I told Ronald vaguely. "What I said earlier."

"Your back?" Ronald guessed.

"Uh-huh. There."

"And how long have you had it?" he persisted.

I sighed. "Oh, I don't know. A month or two? I don't really remember."

Mom must have started wondering what I was talking to Ronald about. She glanced up again with a curious little frown.

"A month or two?" Ronald yelped, sounding worried. "That's a long time! Are you sure it's nothing serious?"

I heard the faint sound of the front door opening and slamming shut again. A second later Elizabeth streaked past the kitchen doorway, heading for the stairs. She didn't even stop in to say hello and let Mom know she was home, like she usually does.

"I've got to go now, Ronald," I said, keeping my voice as polite as possible so Mom wouldn't freak out. "Elizabeth just got home, and it looks like she really needs someone to talk to. See you tomorrow, okay?"

I hung up before he could protest or ask any more questions about my imaginary rash. "Jessica . . . ," Mom began, but I didn't give her a chance to finish.

"Later, Mom. I'd better go see what's wrong with Lizzie," I said, and ran upstairs as fast as I could.

Anna

My mother stayed in the bathtub for almost an hour and a half. That's one of the easiest ways to tell how she's feeling. On her good days she mostly just takes a shower. But on bad days she spends as much time as possible soaking in the tub.

I sat on the floor in the hall outside the bathroom, hugging my knees and pressing my back to the wall as I waited for her to finish. The downstairs toilet still wasn't working right, even though the plumber had been out to our house about a million times in the past few weeks. While I waited, I thought about all that idiotic stuff I'd written to Salvador. What was I thinking? I guess the answer was that I *wasn't* thinking—not clearly anyway. My head was so full of Tim these days that I couldn't fit anything else inside, like common sense or rational thoughts.

"Hey, sweetie, what are you doing?"

I glanced up at my dad standing over me, his face creased with concern.

"I'm just, you know, waiting," I explained, gesturing behind me. Dad stared past me at the closed bathroom door, the lines in his face seeming to deepen. My heart started pounding as I wondered if he would say something this time, about how crazy our home had become.

Finally his eyes moved back to my face, and I almost thought I could see tears. Then he tilted his head slightly, and they were gone. *Just the light,* I realized bitterly.

He cleared his throat. "This is a rough time for us, I know," he said quietly, shuffling his feet on the wooden floor.

Wait—was he actually *admitting* that? Out loud?

"Why don't you and I, uh, get some ice cream together tomorrow? I can get out of work a little early."

I stared up at him. Maybe he *was* ready to face what time of year it was, out in the open. "Yeah, sure," I told him.

A slight smile flitted across his lips, and then he turned and walked into the master bedroom, closing the door behind him.

I was still stunned from the whole exchange when Mom finally emerged into the hall, wrapped in her favorite bathrobe—the red chenille one that Tim gave her for Mother's Day a few years ago.

She almost walked right by, but then she stopped and blinked down at me. "Hi, honey," she said in that distant voice that meant she wasn't all there. Her eyes were blurry and unfocused, like she was looking *in* instead of *out*. "It's getting late. You'd better get some sleep."

I glanced at my watch. It was only eight-fifteen. But I nodded. "Okay, Mom," I said softly. "Good night."

She drifted down the hall. A second later I heard the master bedroom click shut once more.

When she was gone, I hurried into the bathroom and locked the door behind me. It was so damp and steamy after Mom's bath that it felt like a rain forest could grow in there, but I didn't mind. All I could think about was that my dad was finally going to *talk* to me about what was happening to us. But I didn't want to get my hopes up. The people in my life were too good at sending major mixed messages.

I pulled the note I'd written to Salvador out of my pocket and stared at it for a minute. Would I ever find out if he wanted to be more than just friends?

I didn't know. But writing stupid notes that made no sense wasn't the best way to accomplish anything. I ripped the paper into itty-bitty shreds and tossed the pieces into the toilet bowl. Pressing down the handle, I watched as they swirled down into oblivion.

Elizabeth

I ran straight up to my room as soon as I got home. I just wasn't in the mood to talk to anybody, not even my family. I needed to do some serious thinking in private first.

Almost as soon as I'd locked my bedroom door behind me, someone rattled the doorknob. "Lizzie?" Jessica's voice sounded muffled through the door. "What are you doing in there?"

"I'm busy," I called back. I tossed my notebook in the general direction of my desk and flopped onto my bed. "I need to work on my article. I promised I'd have it ready by tomorrow." That much was true enough, although just at the moment I couldn't even bear the thought of walking into the *Zone* meeting and facing Salvador and Anna.

The doorknob rattled again, harder this time. "What? I can't hear you. Let me in."

I ignored her, hoping she'd get bored and go away. The doorknob stopped jangling. *Thank God*, I thought. I stared at the ceiling from my spot on the bed, wondering how my life had gotten so confusing.

Then the bathroom door flew open and Jessica hurried in. I groaned. The bathroom connects my room to Jessica's room, and I'd forgotten to lock that door.

"Hi, Lizzie," Jessica said cheerfully. She flung herself onto the bed beside me. "You'll never guess who I was talking to just now when you came in."

"Huh?" My head was still spinning. *Why did I kiss Salvador back?* I asked myself in agony. *Why am I still thinking about how nice our kiss was?*

I felt a hard poke on my arm. "Hey!" Jessica said loudly. "Did you hear what I just said?"

"Ouch!" I rubbed my arm where she'd poked me. "Why'd you do that?"

"Because," Jessica said impatiently, "I'm trying to tell you that I was talking to Ronald Rheece on the phone—that's *Ronald Rheece*—and you didn't even blink. You're not under the impression that I'm actually *friends* with him, are you?"

"I don't know," I said helplessly. I kept remembering how Salvador had looked just before he'd kissed me. But every time I pictured his black eyes gazing down at me, I also imagined Anna's brown eyes glaring at me accusingly. The three of us had a great friendship. A simple friends-only friendship. How could I ruin it like this?

"Listen, Jess. I really have to get to work on my article soon, or I'll never—"

"Article, schmarticle." Jessica rolled her eyes. "Come on, I'm in serious trouble here. It's bad enough that Ronald is my locker partner. But now he's waiting for me after track practice, calling me at home. . . ." She spread her hands helplessly. "Where will it end, Lizzie? Where will it end?"

I definitely wasn't in the mood for one of my twin's social crises just then. "I don't know," I snapped. "And right now, I really don't care."

Jessica looked hurt. "Fine," she said sulkily. "Then go write your stupid article. I'll just have to go figure this out all by myself."

She slunk back to her own room. I felt so guilty that I almost called her back and apologized, but I couldn't quite bring myself to do it.

What's wrong with me these days? I wondered, rolling over and burying my face in my pillow.

To: RadioRon
From: WakefieldSV
Re: Sorry, wrong number
Message:

Dear Ronald, is it? I'm so sorry, but I think there's been some confusion. You seem to be looking for someone named Jessica Wakefield, but you've got the totally wrong e-mail address. My name is Stella von Wakefieldia, and I'm an eighty-five-year-old great-grandmother living in Russia.

I don't know how my e-mail address got into your school's computer. But it's obviously some kind of horrible mistake. And no offense, but please don't try writing to this address again since I like to keep the space open for my fifty-five grandchildren and great-grandchildren. I'm sure you understand.

Good-bye forever,
Stella von Wakefieldia

Salvador

I flopped down onto the sofa in the front parlor, for once hardly noticing how the antique springs poked into my butt and the scratchy old wool fabric made me itch. When I first came to live with the Doña, it was pretty scary to walk around her huge old house with all those antique chairs and vases and things just sitting there waiting to get broken. But I definitely wasn't thinking about that at the moment. All I could think about was Elizabeth.

Our kiss had been totally amazing, just like the first one. A little short, thanks to the Doña, but otherwise practically perfect. The whole evening had been pretty incredible once we'd gotten to the tower. Up there, it was easy to imagine we were the only people in the world.

But we weren't. And as soon as the Doña had interrupted us, things had gone all wrong. As we headed back out to the car, Elizabeth had looked like her favorite hamster had just died. Or maybe her best friend.

Okay, I thought, picking at the sofa cushion, *I can see how she's a little embarrassed at getting caught. But it's not like the Doña started screaming or fainted in shock or anything. She didn't even say anything about it.* I shrugged. *So what's the big deal? Why wouldn't Elizabeth talk to me or even look at me the whole way home? Why did she look so freaked out?*

I sighed and stood up, wandering around in a circle on the oriental rug. Finally I plopped down on the wing chair near the front window.

It's not like you did much to help the situation, Mr. Smooth, I told myself. *As soon as you got a glimpse of that woe-is-me expression on her face, you turned into some kind of zombie.*

The two of us had just sat there in the backseat of the car the whole way home, staring out our own windows, while the Doña hummed along to some crazy marching music she'd found on the radio. When we got to the Wakefields' house, Elizabeth barely mumbled a "thanks for the ride" at the Doña before she leaped out of the car and ran inside.

"Bizarre," I mumbled out loud, standing up and walking over to the sofa again. "Totally bizarre. Like Jekyll and Hyde. Or Wakefield and Weirdo."

I felt a little guilty for that last part. Whatever

might be bothering her, Elizabeth wasn't weird. If either of us had done something wrong, it would definitely have to be me. I only wished I knew what it was so I could fix it.

I leaned back against the sofa's hard wooden frame. Thinking about the evening was like having a movie playing in my head on some kind of endlessly repeating loop. I kept remembering our nice conversation, and then the kiss, and then the interruption, and then that unhappy expression. I must have sat there for at least half an hour, trying to figure out what I'd done wrong. After a while I was vaguely aware that the phone was ringing, but I didn't budge. It stopped after a couple of rings.

"Salvador!" The Doña appeared in the doorway a few seconds later. "Phone call."

My heart leaped. For a second I was sure it was Elizabeth, calling to say that she'd just realized she was crazy about me. *Salvador, you magnificent fellow,* she would say in her softest, most adoring voice. *I'm sorry I acted so weird back there. I couldn't help myself. My emotions were just too strong. But now that I've realized you're the most incredible guy in the world, I want to come over to your house right now so we can kiss some more. I don't even care if your grandmother sees us. . . .*

75

But when I picked up the phone, it wasn't her. It was only Brian.

"Hi," I greeted him dully.

"Hey, man," he said. "What's up with your grandma? I said I was calling to see how the tower thing went, and she started laughing her head off like I said the funniest thing she'd ever heard. What's her deal?"

I gritted my teeth, wishing that the Doña hadn't seen that kiss. "My grandmother has a big mouth," I said grimly. "I'm going to have to speak to her about that right away."

Brian cleared his throat. "Look, if you'd rather not tell me—"

"It's okay," I said quickly. Now that I thought about it, it might be useful to get another guy's opinion. It wasn't as if I could talk to Anna about what had happened or even the Doña. I mean, she's a pretty cool grandmother, but there are limits. "Uh, actually she was talking about me and Elizabeth. While we were at the top of the tower, we sort of—uh, well—kissed."

"You're kidding!" Brian laughed. "Wow. That's what I call in-depth research."

I snorted. "Funny. But that's the good part. The bad part is that I'm not sure what Elizabeth thinks of me."

"What are you talking about? You just said you guys kissed."

"I know." I twisted the phone cord around my finger until I was afraid my circulation was going to get cut off. "But my grandmother caught us, and then on the way home she seemed kind of upset or something."

"Your grandmother?"

I rolled my eyes. "No! Elizabeth." I paused. "I guess I'm still not sure if she likes me. You know—like that."

"Oh." Brian was silent for a moment. "Well, you can't always tell. Girls act weird sometimes, and it can be hard to figure out what they're thinking, you know?"

I did know that. But I was sort of relieved to hear someone else say it. "Thanks," I told Brian. "But listen, you won't say anything about this, right?"

"I won't say a word to anyone," Brian promised. "I swear."

"Thanks." I knew I could count on him. Brian really is a pretty cool guy.

"Well, hang in there," Brian said. "I'll see you at the meeting tomorrow."

I groaned. The *Zone* meeting. Yeah, that was going to be a barrel of laughs. "Okay," I told Brian glumly. "See you."

I hung up the phone and went in search of the Doña. I found her in the kitchen, putting the teakettle on the stove. "Can I talk to you?" I asked her.

"Of course, Salvador." She smiled knowingly as she wiped her hands on a dish towel. "Does this have something to do with a certain young lady named Elizabeth?"

"Sort of," I said, feeling awkward. "Um, but it's more about what you said to Brian just now. You know, about tonight."

She looked surprised. "What did I say?"

"Well, Brian said you *laughed* when he asked about the tower," I started. "I know you didn't mean to see us, but . . ." I trailed off, my ears burning. "See, the problem is that I don't know what that—that"—I couldn't quite bring myself to say the word *kiss* to her—"what it meant," I finished at last. I shrugged. "So I'd really appreciate it if you didn't say anything about it. To *anyone*," I added with extra emphasis as the image of her blabbing to my parents the next time they called floated into my mind.

"All right, all right. I'll try to keep my big mouth shut." The Doña's eyes were still sparkling. She shook her head. "But you need to remember, Salvador. Every action, every choice has consequences. You were in a public place. If you didn't want anyone to know about what you were doing, perhaps you should have chosen somewhere more private."

Just then the teakettle started to whistle, and she turned away to take care of it. That gave me the chance to escape her lecture. I figured it wasn't worth trying to explain that the kiss wasn't part of some great master plan I'd cooked up. It wasn't as if I'd *known* I was going to kiss Elizabeth right then and there. It just *happened.*

Now all I had to figure out was what was going to happen next.

Heights and Sights
Sweet Valley Tower by Moonlight
by Elizabeth Wakefield

All of us have seen the lofty shape of the Sweet Valley Tower rising above our town like a beacon. But how many have actually ridden the elevator to the top and gazed out over the twinkling lights of Sweet Valley by the light of the silvery moon?

Surely the people who built the tower didn't have much time for gazing at the sky. Construction began some fifty years ago during a building spree that revitalized what had been a sleepy small town in a remote valley. Highways were created, linking Sweet Valley to larger towns and cities nearby, including Los Angeles. That brought more people to our town, which meant an increased need for schools, hospitals, shopping facilities, and homes. To celebrate Sweet Valley's popularity boom, then-prominent local businessmen Gregory Monroe Patman and Richard Fowler Sr. decided to give the town's budding skyline a special symbol of its upward progression. And thus the idea for the Sweet Valley Tower was born.

It took a team of more than forty men nearly a year to complete the tower that we all know and love today. During that time the builders used a number of methods and tools that were almost revolutionary in their era, although most seem much more commonplace—or even old-fashioned—today. Components like granite and steel were all key to the construction effort. There's a detailed information board in the lower lobby of the tower for anyone who is interested in more of these fascinating details.

Overall, I would highly recommend a visit to the Sweet Valley Tower as an educational class trip. It's perfect for large groups, and it will give students a whole new perspective on their hometown.

Why Do We Change?
by Anna Wang

I wonder why
People have to change.

I used to count on you
To make me laugh.
And that was enough.

I wonder why
I have to change.

People say that change is good.
I used to agree.
But then *you* changed.

Salvador

I stopped short just inside the doorway to the room where we hold our *Zone* meetings. Elizabeth and Brian were sitting close together, deep in conversation.

I guess I sort of panicked. *Were they talking about the kiss?* I rushed right over. "Hi!" I almost shouted. "Talking about me?"

Brian's eyes widened. "No!" he replied instantly. "Of course not. Why would we be talking about you?"

Elizabeth shot him a slightly suspicious glance, then looked back at me, her eyes narrow. "We were just trying to figure out how many pages we should make the first issue of the 'zine," she said.

I gulped, distracted by how pretty she looked. She was wearing a blue shirt that made her eyes look the same color as the ocean on a sunny day. Also, I couldn't seem to stop staring at her lips.

"Oh," I said. "Um, okay." I hoped she

hadn't figured out that Brian knew about the kiss.

"Hey!" Brian said suddenly. "Here's Anna. I guess we can get this meeting started."

I turned to glance at the door, where Anna was just coming in. She looked kind of grim. I did my best to pull myself together and act normal as Elizabeth called the meeting to order.

The Meeting

3:30 P.M.   As the *Zone* meeting begins, Elizabeth and Salvador both start talking at the same time. Both of them stop immediately and politely insist the other one go first. "No, you first," Elizabeth says. Salvador shakes his head. "Please, I insist. I'd rather hear what *you* have to say." This continues until Anna puts her hands on her hips and interrupts, saying if neither of them wants to talk, *she'll* go first. Brian laughs uncharacteristically loudly.

3:34 P.M.   Brian suggests an idea for interviewing former students about their experiences in junior high. "They could tell it like it really is," he says. "You know, like one of those kiss-and-tell articles in girls' magazines." Realizing what he's said, he glances at Elizabeth and Salvador and laughs awkwardly. "Or, you know, not."

3:35 P.M.   Elizabeth begins to suspect that Salvador has told Brian about the kiss. She is so angry that she can't see straight. But she can't do anything about it now without letting Anna in on the secret too. So she swallows her anger and concentrates on surviving the meeting without exploding—or leaping out of her chair and strangling Salvador.

3:38 P.M.   "Okay," Elizabeth says, trying to get the meeting back on track. "I know it's kind of a lame idea, but my sister made me promise to suggest we do a hair-and-make-out column."

Brian laughs and then slaps a hand over his mouth to stop himself. Anna looks surprised. "*What* kind of column?" she says.

Elizabeth sees that Salvador is blushing furiously. She wonders what she said.

Brian takes his hand away from his mouth. "I think you mean a hair-and-make*up* column, right, Elizabeth?"

3:41 P.M.   Anna is wishing they could finish the meeting already so she could go home. She is feeling more depressed than ever about her brother and very anxious about her plans with her father. She was hoping that being with her friends would distract her. But all they're doing is annoying her by acting like freaks. Can't she count on anything in her life being normal anymore?

3:49 P.M.   Elizabeth hands out copies of her Sweet Valley Tower article to read. Anna scans it quickly. "No offense, Elizabeth, but this is kind of boring," she says. "I thought the point was to make it sound like a romantic place for a date. You know, with the moonlight and all."

"Moonlight?" Salvador says loudly. "What's so romantic about some stupid old moonlight?"

"I don't think anyone cares about that kind of romance and dating stuff," Brian adds. "Besides, I thought the part about the construction methods was really interesting."

Elizabeth nods. "People really care about construction methods. Construction methods are much more important than moonlight."

Anna wonders if they have all been possessed by aliens.

3:52 P.M.   Elizabeth gets up to sharpen her pencil and accidentally brushes against Salvador's arm as she walks by. Her face turns red, and he starts coughing uncontrollably. Brian pretends to choke on a piece of gum to keep Anna from noticing. All Anna notices is that the three of them are acting more idiotic by the minute.

3:55 P.M. Anna brings up the tower article again. She really thinks they need to discuss it more. "Don't you think it could use a little more action?" she asks.

Brian laughs loudly for a second, then stops when Elizabeth turns bright red and punches him on the arm. This time Salvador pretends to choke on *his* gum, even though he's not chewing any.

Anna can't take their bizarre behavior anymore. She storms out of the room, close to tears.

Elizabeth

I stared after Anna in shock. I had been so busy trying to stop myself from doing something totally embarrassing, like killing Salvador or blurting out another accidental comment about making out, that her sudden exit took me completely by surprise.

I guess the others were stunned too because for a long moment nobody said a word. Finally Brian cleared his throat.

"Whoa," he said. "She looked pretty upset."

Salvador nodded. "Um, I wonder why?"

Brian gave him a disgusted look. Then he glanced at me. "Give me a break," he said to both of us. "You two aren't exactly great actors, you know. Even my eight-year-old sister could figure out that something's up between you. Obviously Anna noticed too, and it looks like she's upset about it." He shrugged. "So maybe you ought to tell her about what happened last night, before she starts feeling even worse about being left out."

"I don't know what you're—," I started to protest before Salvador interrupted me.

"But . . . I . . . you . . ." he choked out in this tight, strangled voice. His face was turning lobster red.

Brian shook his head. He looked really annoyed. "I know I promised not to say anything," he said. "But this is ridiculous. Anna's your friend, right?"

"Right." Salvador's voice still didn't sound too normal.

I saw what Brian was getting at. "You're right, Brian," I said, my own voice coming out kind of shaky. I wasn't sure if it was anger at Salvador or nervousness about Anna that was making it sound that way. But I cleared my throat and tried to sound firmer. "Anna's our friend, and we should tell her the truth." I risked a quick glance at Salvador. "She deserves to know."

Brian nodded. He turned to Salvador. "Well?"

Salvador said something that sounded like, "Ulp." But then he nodded too. "Okay. I guess." He still didn't sound too certain.

As annoyed as I was at him at the moment, I didn't blame him. Anna had looked really upset just now. And I still remembered how she'd freaked out when she had first found out that Salvador liked me as more than a friend.

Are we more than friends now? I wondered, peeking at him again. I was so mad at him for blabbing to Brian right now and so worried about Anna that I wasn't sure. *Do I want us to be more than friends?*

Straightening up in my chair, I did my best to push those thoughts aside. First things first. "Do you want to tell her?" I asked Salvador. "I mean, you guys have been friends for a long time and everything. . . ."

He looked sort of panicky at the suggestion. "Um, I don't know," he said. "Maybe we should go talk to her together."

Brian shook his head firmly. "Bad idea," he announced.

Salvador looked a little insulted. "What do you mean?"

"Think about it," Brian said. "Anna's already feeling left out, right? How's it going to look if the two of you go see her together—you know, like, as a couple?"

"You're right," I agreed quickly, glad that someone at least was thinking straight. Seeing that Salvador still looked nervous, I added, "I'll go talk to her first, if you want." I wasn't sure what I was going to say, but I figured I'd come up with something. Salvador had been acting pretty immature all day—I wasn't sure he could handle this right now. And we couldn't afford to mess things up with Anna any more than we already had. Not if we all wanted to stay friends.

Salvador looked relieved. "Really?" he said. "You don't mind?"

I shook my head, not meeting his eye, and stood up. "I guess this means this *Zone* meeting is adjourned." Taking a deep breath, I headed for the door.

Jessica

"Ready to go, Jessica?" my friend Bethel asked as I was putting my regular shoes back on after track practice. "I'll walk out with you."

"Um . . ." My mind was racing. I was positive that a certain lovesick science nerd was waiting for me outside the gym. And I definitely didn't want Bethel or any of my other friends from the track team to see him there and get the wrong idea. But what was I supposed to do? Hang around in the locker room until it got dark, hoping he'd give up and go home?

Bethel raised an eyebrow and stared at me. "Well?" she demanded. "It's a simple question, Wakefield. Are you ready to go or not?"

Ginger Walters glanced over at us and laughed. Even Mary Stillwater smiled a little.

I blushed as I realized I was sitting there with my mouth hanging open as I tried to decide what to say. Clamping my lips shut, I smiled brightly at Bethel. "Not quite," I told her. "Uh, I mean, I forgot something in my locker. So I'll have to go out the back way and get it." I jumped to my feet, realizing just how brilliant my spur-of-the-moment excuse was. If I walked out through the school instead of straight through the gym doors like I usually did, I wouldn't have to pass Ronald's lurking spot at all. And if Bethel and the others saw him, they would probably just think he was standing there counting blades of grass for some calculus project or something. "See you tomorrow, okay?"

I heard Bethel and some of my other teammates call "bye" after me as I hurried toward the locker-room door.

That was a close one, I thought as I was making my way through the interior gym doors. Then a terrible idea occurred to me. *What if Ronald asks Bethel where I am? Or worse, he asks her if my rash is getting any better!*

But if Ronald was lurking outside the gym, it was best to avoid him at all costs. I just had to pray that he wouldn't let anyone know he was looking for me.

I hurried down the hall. I'd avoided my admirer all day by steering clear of our locker. That meant I had to carry every single one of my books around with me all day. As well as my lunch *and* my gym stuff. Still, desperate times call for desperate measures.

My arms already felt about three inches longer from dragging around that weight all day, so I figured I might as well actually stop at my locker. I could drop off the books for today's classes and pick up the ones I'd need tomorrow so I wouldn't have to go near the locker at all tomorrow morning. I was seriously thinking I might never use my locker again. At least not during actual school hours.

I turned and headed in that direction.

The hallway was almost empty, except for some stragglers just getting out of their activities. I sighed, slowing down my pace and enjoying the sensation of moving freely through the school. As I was passing by the door to the *Spec* office, it burst open and people started pouring out. I stepped back to avoid being caught up in the throng of kids.

Then I recognized the gorgeous short, brown hair and deep blue eyes I'd been daydreaming about so often lately. . . .

"Damon," I whispered, stopping.

He spotted me and smiled his usual warm, friendly grin. I gulped, smiling back as he approached.

"Hey, Jessica," he said cheerfully. "What're you up to?"

I blushed. *Oh, just the usual. You know, walking*

to my locker after hours to avoid a run-in with a lovesick dork who apparently has me confused with someone who enjoys being stalked.

"Nothing, really," I muttered, shrugging. "You had a *Spec* meeting?"

He nodded, staring at me so intently, I felt my palms start to sweat. He seemed sort of on edge. Was he actually—*finally*—going to ask me out?

"Yeah, I haven't been at too many meetings lately, but I guess they're not ready to get rid of me yet," he joked, stuffing his hands in his pockets. "So, Jess, I wanted to—"

"Jessica!" a voice exclaimed. "Hey, Jessica!"

I froze. My mind totally refused to accept what I was hearing.

"R-Ronald?" I stammered, turning around.

"What good timing," Ronald said, grinning like a maniac. "My meeting just ended."

"Meeting?" I repeated stupidly. I glanced at Damon, whose brow was knit in confusion. *What were you about to ask me, Damon?* I wondered in agony.

Ronald nodded. "The Future Scientists of America club," he explained.

Looking past him, I saw half a dozen other fashion-challenged students coming out of a classroom farther down the hallway.

This has got to be some kind of nightmare, I

decided. *It couldn't possibly be real. It's just too humiliating. The only thing worse would be if I suddenly noticed I was walking around naked.*

With a flash of nervousness, I gazed down at myself. Fortunately I was still fully clothed. Or maybe it wasn't so fortunate since it meant this whole horrible scene was all too real.

Ronald blushed, looking sort of embarrassed. "Anyway," he said loudly. "It was a very interesting meeting."

"Really?" I said automatically.

"I'd better get going," Damon broke in. I whipped my head around, restraining myself from physically grabbing his arm and begging him not to leave. "I'll see you later, Jessica." He flashed one of his heart-melting smiles, nodded quickly to Ronald, then hurried off.

"We spent most of the time discussing quarks," Ronald continued, as if this information actually mattered to me. "You know, because of the lecture tonight at the university."

"Huh?" I had no idea what he was talking about. I was busy contemplating the fact that Ronald had just ruined my first shot with the guy I'd been drooling over since the beginning of school. I glanced quickly down the hall toward the entrance, wondering if I should just make a break for it. After all, I was on the track team. I could definitely outrun Ronald.

"The science lecture," Ronald explained. "At Sweet Valley University. It's tonight. At eight-thirty. It should be *really* interesting."

Suddenly I snapped back into sharp focus. The lecture. The thrilling scientific lecture he'd been blabbing about for the past week. It was tonight. And I guessed, with a sinking feeling, that he was about to invite me to go with him. On a date. To learn about quarks.

I couldn't let it happen. But with my luck, even if I said no, my parents would find out about it and force me to go anyway. They'd probably make me sign up for the Future Scientists of America while I was at it. Besides, Ronald was so—so *helpless*. So little and nerdy and trusting. How could I stand there and break his heart by turning him down flat?

All of that flashed through my mind in about half a second. And I guess I sort of panicked.

"Excuse me," I blurted out. "Um, I've got to go. To the bathroom." He couldn't follow me there.

"Oh." Ronald looked a little embarrassed again, but he nodded. "Okay, don't worry. I'll wait for you right here."

"No!" I yelled. He looked startled, and I gulped, realizing I was probably sounding a little

crazy. "Um, it's my stomach. I might be a while."
Remembering a repulsive chapter from last year's
biology textbook, I added, "I think I might have
a tapeworm. I'll probably be throwing up for the
next hour or two."

Ronald looked even more startled at that, but
I didn't stick around to watch. I raced for the
girls' room.

Once safely inside, I collapsed against the
wall near the row of sinks. *Now what am I going
to do?* I wondered, letting my backpack slide to
the floor beside me. *How long am I going to have
to hide out in here?*

I had to get serious about this problem. For
one thing, I knew that even if I managed to escape today, I would still have to deal with
Ronald again tomorrow. He wasn't the type of
guy to give up on a lost cause. His wardrobe was
proof of that. And he didn't seem to have the
slightest clue that someone like me was totally
out of his league. So unless I wanted to spend
the rest of the eighth grade in the girls' bathroom—or live with the guilt of scarring Ronald
for life by telling him the truth—I needed to
come up with a plan.

While I was thinking about it, I wandered
over to the sink and pulled out my lip gloss and
a hairbrush. There was no sense letting all those

mirrors go to waste. After slicking a layer of Perfectly Peachy on my lips, I tossed the gloss back in my backpack and grabbed the brush. I leaned forward, flipped my hair over the front of my head, and started brushing it out from the roots to make it look fuller.

Maybe it was all the blood rushing to my head. I don't know. But I suddenly had a flash of inspiration.

Of course! I thought, almost dropping my brush at the obviousness of it all. *There's only one sure way to get Ronald to leave me alone. I have to set him up with another girl.*

I flipped my hair back into its usual place and stood up straight. As far as I could tell, there was just one flaw in the idea. But, I realized, it was a huge one. What girl would possibly be interested in a science-obsessed nerd like Ronald?

I bit my lip, ready to abandon the plan.

Then something occurred to me. *I don't really need to find a girl who's actually interested in Ronald,* I told myself, still gazing at my reflection. *I just have to find a girl Ronald likes better than me. Then he'll leave me alone for good, and I'll have a chance at a normal social life!* I winced as I remembered how fast Damon had booked when Ronald showed up. *That is, as long as Damon doesn't avoid me forever after seeing old Ronnie talk to me like we're best friends!*

I shook my head slightly, admiring the way the fluorescent lights of the bathroom made my bouncy new waves shimmer. Then I sighed. Ronald was totally into me. Who could I possibly find who could take my place in his heart?

Frustrated, I ran both hands over my hair, smoothing out all the body I'd just given it. I held my hands there for a second. Maybe if I squeezed my own head hard enough, an answer would come to me.

And it did. With my hair held back from my face like that and my face almost free of makeup, I looked exactly like . . . Elizabeth!

"Perfect," I murmured.

A n n a

I glanced down at my watch the second I noticed Dad's car missing from the driveway. When I saw how late it was, I felt a lump form in my throat. *He forgot.*

I went inside, slamming the door behind me. The sound resounded through the house. On the desk in the living room the answering machine's red light was blinking. I dropped my book bag and went over to it. As soon as I pressed play, my dad's voice filled the room.

"Hi, honey," he started hollowly. "I'm sorry about today, but I'm not going to be able to get out of work after all. See you tonight." Click.

So he didn't forget—he just couldn't face me.

I sank onto the couch. Even though I knew Mom was upstairs—probably locked in the bedroom or soaking in the tub—I felt lonelier than ever. Tears streamed down my face, and I grabbed a cushion and began to sob into it.

Almost an hour passed. I was still lying there in the dark, crying like I'd just learned how to do it. And then I heard the doorbell ring.

For the first three buzzes I just lay there and stared up at the ceiling, waiting for the noise to stop. But whoever it was wasn't giving up easily. When the fourth ring came, I groaned and dragged myself to my feet.

Maybe it's Salvador, I thought with a tiny spark of hope. *Maybe he finally woke up and realized what month this is. Maybe he's coming to apologize for forgetting.* I sniffled loudly. *And maybe I'll even forgive him, if he begs hard enough.*

Walking slowly to the mirror in the front hall, I checked out my reflection. I looked even worse than I felt, if that was possible. My eyes were red and puffy. My skin was sallow, blotchy, and streaked with dried tears. My hair was a matted mess.

"Who cares?" I said out loud to my reflection. "Who cares what I look like? Who cares about anything?"

Still, I did try to wipe at least some of the snot off my face with my sleeve as I stumbled toward the entrance. Just as the bell buzzed for the third time, I swung open the door.

But it wasn't Salvador. It was Elizabeth.

"Anna!" she exclaimed. "What's the matter? You look awful."

I almost slammed the door shut again, right

in her worried face. But something made me hesitate. Elizabeth looked so kind, so concerned. Like she really cared about what I was going through, even though she had no way of knowing exactly what that was. Even though she hadn't even known me when Tim . . .

"Anna?" She took a step forward. "Can I come in?"

I still wasn't sure what to say or do. But suddenly I knew I didn't want to be alone anymore. "Um, okay," I said, stepping back to let her enter.

I led the way back to the living room, snapping on the overhead light on the way. Elizabeth followed and waited until I sat down on the couch. Then she sat down next to me.

"Anna?" she said softly. "Do you want to talk about it?"

"Um . . ." I thought I was going to say no. But I couldn't quite get the word out. I suddenly felt like I really wanted to talk to Elizabeth right now. I needed to talk to *someone*.

And it's not like there's anyone else here applying for the job, I thought bitterly. My eyes wandered to the card Salvador had left me the day before. It was standing on the coffee table a few feet away.

"Yes," I told Elizabeth, blinking back a few more tears. "I think I would like to talk about it." I took a deep breath. "The reason I've been so upset lately—it's because it's almost the anniversary of when my—my older brother died."

Elizabeth gasped. "Oh, Anna!" Her blue-green eyes filled with tears, and she leaned over and hugged me tight. "I'm sorry. I had no idea."

I hugged her back. It felt kind of good. I didn't know if it was the hug itself or just the relief of saying what I was feeling out loud. "I've been thinking about him all the time lately," I said, my voice a little muffled by her shoulder. "And I'm really feeling sad. You know, remembering. . . . Anyway, I guess the way you guys were acting at that *Zone* meeting today kind of put me over the edge. I mean, I've been sort of out of it anyway because of Tim, and then today you were all cracking up. . . . I felt really left out."

Elizabeth hugged me even tighter. "I understand," she said. "We were acting like jerks. It's okay now."

After a few more seconds I pulled away. I still felt heavy and sad inside, but not quite as completely hopeless as I'd been before she'd arrived. It was sort of the feeling I got after I finished a poem. Like I'd managed to chip away at some of my sadness by getting it out from inside me.

"Thanks," I said, suddenly shy. I'd never shared anything so personal with Elizabeth before, and it felt sort of like a new step in our friendship. "Thanks for listening."

"Anytime." She reached over and gently pushed back a strand of hair that had fallen into my face.

I started feeling self-conscious about how horrible I looked. It didn't help that Elizabeth looked perfectly beautiful, like always. "Excuse me," I said with a sniffle. "I want to go splash some cold water on my face."

She nodded, and I stood up and hurried to the bathroom. Turning on the tap, I stuck my whole head down in the sink and splashed vigorously for as long as I could hold my breath.

Then I stood and rubbed my face on a towel until my skin tingled. Tossing the towel back on the rack, I stared at myself in the mirror. *Who would have guessed that Elizabeth would be the one who would try to help?* I thought in amazement. *After all, she never even met Tim.* I shrugged. *Still, I guess that's what friends are for, right? To be there for you no matter what.*

I pushed open the bathroom door and headed back to the living room. When I got there, Elizabeth had something in her hand. She glanced up quickly when she heard me enter.

"Oops!" she said with a little laugh. "Sorry, I'm clumsy. I knocked this card off the table, and I was just putting it back."

"That's okay. No big deal." It was the bat card

from Salvador, and I couldn't help feeling a little embarrassed. I mean, it's not like having a silly bat-shaped card sitting around your house is totally normal. But luckily she didn't seem to be looking at the card. She was staring at me, and her face looked so sad that I almost felt guilty for depressing her so much.

"Anna, I'm really sorry, but I need to go," she said apologetically. "Will you be all right by yourself?"

I nodded. "I'm okay," I said with a tiny smile. "Now."

She smiled back, still looking sad. Then, after one more quick hug, she hurried out of the house.

After she left, I went back to the couch and stretched out on it. I won't say I was feeling totally better—after all, it wasn't like anything had really changed. Tim was still gone. I was still lonely.

But at least this time I left the lights on.

Elizabeth

Anna's sad face stayed in my mind as I hurried toward Salvador's house. It wasn't a very long walk from Anna's place to his, so I didn't have much time to figure out what I was going to say to him. Salvador and I had been so wrapped up in ourselves that we hadn't even noticed how badly Anna was hurting. We were so stupid. And blind.

No, I told myself as I quickened my pace. *You were blind because you didn't know.* Salvador *was stupid.*

I hadn't told Anna about the kiss—I didn't think I ever would. She was miserable, and we'd been incredibly selfish. I was so angry with Salvador, I could barely walk straight. I took a deep breath as I stepped up onto Salvador's front porch. The door flew open before I raised my hand to lift the knocker.

"Elizabeth!" Salvador grinned cheesily. "That was quick. I've been going crazy wondering how it was going. I even started biting my nails. See?"

He stepped out onto the porch and thrust his hands under my nose. I pushed them away impatiently. "Salvador. Listen."

I don't know if he actually heard me or not because he just kept talking. "I can't believe we've been so stupid and secretive all this time. We should have just told Anna in the first place. Then we might already be—well, you know—kind of going out or whatever."

"No!" My voice came out louder than I'd expected. It was so loud that it actually shut him up. I swallowed hard. "I didn't tell her."

"What?" Salvador looked stunned. "What do you mean, you didn't tell her?"

"I mean I didn't tell her. I couldn't." I shuffled my feet on the wooden floor of the porch, crossing my arms over my chest. "When I got there, I found out she wasn't upset because of us after all. She told me it's almost the anniversary of when her brother died." I stopped, watching as his face started to turn pale. "That's why she's been so sad lately," I said icily.

"Oh!" Salvador gasped and stepped backward, his body seeming to sag before my eyes. "That's right. I guess . . . I forgot."

Forgot? What kind of a friend is he?

I took a deep breath. "While I was over there, I saw a card you gave her."

109

"What?" Salvador frowned for a moment. Then he got an *aha* look on his face. "Oh, right. That silly bat."

"I don't think she thought it was silly," I said, gritting my teeth. How could he be so dense? "She had it sitting on the table right next to her when I was there."

I wasn't sure I could describe how I'd felt when I'd seen that card. It had been sort of an accident. I really had knocked it off the table, like I'd told Anna. But when I was picking it up, it had fallen open, and I recognized Salvador's handwriting. I didn't plan to read it, but it was so short that my eyes had already scanned it before I realized it was private.

That was when I knew for sure there was absolutely no way I could tell Anna about Salvador and me. She needed all her friends around to help her. Especially Salvador, her best friend. The friend she counted on the most. The friend who hadn't been there for her lately because he'd been too busy kissing me on top of towers . . .

"So," Salvador said awkwardly. "When are you gonna, you know, tell her? About us, I mean."

"I'm not," I blurted out, rage filling me. I took a shaky breath. "In fact, there can't ever *be* an us."

Salvador frowned. "Wait a minute," he

protested. He reached out and pulled the house door shut behind him, leaving the two of us huddled on the porch. "I thought we weren't going to keep secrets from her anymore. That's what you said before, right?"

I tried to control my trembling the best I could. Screaming at Salvador wouldn't do Anna any good, and I wanted both of us to stay focused on Anna right now. That was the least we could do after the way we'd betrayed her. "The most important thing right now is helping Anna," I said grimly. "Making her feel better."

"Okay, okay. But what does that have to do with—you know, the other stuff?" he asked. He reached his hand toward me, as if to touch my arm. "I mean, we could still—"

"No." I jerked my arm away. Why couldn't he see the problem without hearing me spell it out? "We already know how she feels about that. We can't do anything to hurt her more when she's already feeling so terrible about her brother."

I clenched my fists at my sides and took a deep breath. He certainly wasn't making this any easier. Didn't he understand what I was telling him? Didn't he realize this was hard for me too? "Look," I said, carefully keeping my voice neutral. "Anna needs us right now. She especially needs *you*. You're her best friend. So I think you ought to go over there right away and see if she wants to talk."

"Oh, really?" Salvador said sarcastically. "Well, if *you* think that's what I should do, I guess I'd better hop to it."

"What's that supposed to mean?"

He shrugged. "Forget it. Just forget it, okay?"

Before I knew what was happening, he'd pushed past me and jumped off the porch without bothering with the steps. "Salvador . . . ," I began.

But he didn't turn around. He jogged down the walk and turned toward Anna's house without a backward glance.

Jessica's Plan to Subvert Ronald

5:41 P.M.   Jessica is lying in wait when Elizabeth gets home from Salvador's house. "Surprise!" she cries. "Lizzie, have I got an educational treat of a lifetime for you!"

"I'm not in the mood," Elizabeth mutters, pushing past her and running up to her room.

5:42 P.M.   Jessica bursts into Elizabeth's room. Elizabeth is lying facedown on her bed. Jessica pokes her on the butt until she rolls over. "Lizzie, listen to me. . . ."

"Why does your T-shirt have all those dirty black smudges on it?" Elizabeth asks.

Jessica barely glances down. "Oh, it's nothing," she explains. "I had to climb out the bathroom window at school. Um, it was an exercise for track practice."

That actually gets Elizabeth's attention, and she sits up.

5:44 P.M.   Jessica spends several minutes describing how smart and interesting Ronald is. Elizabeth cocks her head

disbelievingly and finally interrupts. "Wait a minute," she says.
"Isn't this the same guy you've been
calling Supreme Overlord King
Nerd of All Nerds?"

Jessica shrugs and grins weakly.
"That was before I got to know
him."

5:50 P.M.   Jessica stomps around her own
room, annoyed because her twin
won't even consider going to the
lecture with Ronald that evening.
Not even when Jessica carefully explained how much homework she
has, which is the only reason she's
not taking advantage of this won-
derful opportunity herself. And not
even when she reminded Elizabeth
that she (Elizabeth, that is) actually
likes science.

5:59 P.M.   Elizabeth gets her old teddy bear
out of the closet and hugs it tightly.
She wonders why things have to be
so complicated for her and Salvador.
Then she thinks about Anna's
brother, and she feels even sadder.
When tears start to trickle down
her face and drip onto the soft

brown bear, she's not sure whether she's crying for Anna or for herself. Or maybe both.

6:15 P.M. As Jessica heads downstairs for dinner, she vows to figure out a way to change Elizabeth's mind. After all, it's her (Jessica's, that is) only chance for a successful, happy junior-high-school career. Otherwise she figures she'll just have to resign herself to being Supreme Overlord Queen Nerd of All Nerds. And she's *definitely* not ready to do that.

Salvador

It's amazing what half an hour of hurling stones into the nearest body of water can do for your state of mind.

After I'd left Elizabeth standing there on my porch, I had started toward Anna's house. But I was so upset that I figured maybe I should wait a few minutes and cool off before I went over there. So I turned and headed for this little park nearby. There's a pond there with a beach full of smooth, flattened-out stones that are just perfect for skipping. So that's what I did. I sat right down at the edge of the water and skipped stones across the pond until my arm started to hurt.

By the time I stopped, I wouldn't say I felt *better,* exactly. *Better* is too strong a word. But at least I no longer felt like my head was about to explode into a million bloody fragments. I figured that was a start.

This sucks. This really sucks, I thought, grabbing one last pebble and winging it over the water. It only skipped twice before it sank under the surface. *Why did I have to end up liking someone like Elizabeth Wakefield anyway? It's not fair.*

My blood boiled when I thought about the stuff she'd said back there. It was totally obvious that however she felt about me, it wasn't even close to how I felt about her. Otherwise she wouldn't be able to just turn off her feelings like that. I wanted her to want to be together no matter what, just like I did.

Not that I'm sure that's even what I want anymore, I thought angrily, shoving my hands in my pockets and kicking at the stones as I turned and headed up off the rocky little beach. *Not after standing there listening to her lecture me about what I should and shouldn't do. Treating me like she was a grown-up talking to some slow little kid.*

Of course, that didn't mean she wasn't partly right. At least about going to see Anna. I felt pretty lousy about forgetting Tim. He and Anna were really close, and her whole family had been a wreck ever since that horrible night. I didn't need Elizabeth Wakefield to tell me how much Anna was hurting right now.

I couldn't get Elizabeth's words out of my mind. How could she just call off our whole . . . thing? Whatever it was. How could she be that way after our last kiss? Hadn't she felt the sparks?

"I guess not," I muttered as I stomped up to Anna's front door. Jabbing at the doorbell, I scowled at the ground.

I forgot all about Elizabeth the minute Anna opened the door. It was obvious that she'd been crying pretty much nonstop all afternoon. She looked like a total mess, and I felt another huge stab of guilt.

"Salvador," she whispered when she saw me. A tear trickled out of the corner of her eye and down her cheek.

"Hi." I cleared my throat. I've always hated seeing her cry. She looks so helpless when she does, like a tiny, scared little girl. "Um, can I come in? I thought you might need some company."

"Really?" She looked a tiny bit suspicious, which made me feel even worse.

I nodded. "Really. I know I've probably seemed a little out of it lately. But I don't want you to think I forgot about you. Or about Tim."

That did it. She stepped back and let me in, and for the next half hour or so, I mostly just rubbed her back and let her sob all over my nice, clean T-shirt. I listened to her talk about Tim, and suddenly I realized I missed him a whole lot too.

"Remember when he would drive us to the movie theater over at the Red Bird Mall sometimes?" I asked. "You know, how he'd tease us the whole time about how at least nobody he knew would see him hanging out with a couple of twerps like us?"

Anna looked at me, her eyes starting to brighten.

"And remember when we slept out in that tent in your backyard?" I continued softly. "And he'd tell us scary stories until we couldn't sleep at all? Then when we were finally starting to fall asleep, he'd come back out and scare us again?"

"He came up with a different way every time," Anna jumped in, a small smile appearing on her lips.

I nodded. One time he played spooky noises on a tape recorder from the other side of the neighbors' fence, and another time he crept up and silently removed all the support pins so the tent collapsed right on top of us. Once he just jumped into the tent yelling. Each time we could never *really* be sure it was him, and we always ended up almost peeing our pajama pants. It was great. *He* was great.

"See?" I told Anna gently, pushing her hair out of her face. A big hunk of it had sort of gotten stuck in a patch of dried tears on her cheek. I peeled it free and tucked it behind her ear. "It's nice to remember the good stuff, right? Not just the bad stuff."

She let out a noisy sniffle and nodded. "You're right." Her voice was shaky and sort of thick, as if all her tears were clogging up her throat. "I'm so glad you came over, Salvador. I—I guess I really needed someone to talk to about this."

"Yeah," I said. "Um, I know you already talked to Elizabeth before. But I figured I—"

"Oh, that's not the same." Anna wiped her nose with the back of her hand and sniffed again. She smiled wanly. "I mean, it was nice talking to her. But she's not—I mean, it wasn't the same as talking to you like this." She shrugged. "I didn't really feel like I could say just anything, like I can with you."

That made me feel pretty good. Partly because it's nice to be needed. And partly because I was still mad at Elizabeth and it was good to know that Anna liked me best.

"You know," Anna went on, her voice sounding weepier again, "no matter how nice she is, it's just different. She never even met Tim."

"I know." I rubbed her shoulder, wincing as I saw the tears trickle down her face. "Don't cry, Anna. It's okay. I'm here," I told her softly. "Do you want a glass of water or something? I could go get you one." I started to stand up.

She shook her head quickly, clinging to my shoulders with both hands. "Don't go," she whispered. "Please."

Her voice broke a little on the words, and I almost couldn't stand it. "I won't go anywhere," I promised, gazing into her face, wishing it didn't look so sad. "I'll stay right here with you."

All I was aware of was an overwhelming desire to make everything better for her. She was looking at me. Her arms were around me. . . . It made perfect sense that I should lean forward a little more to kiss her on the forehead—once, twice, then once more. And it was totally natural that she should tilt her head back slightly. That our lips should brush each other's, move away, then meet again . . .

Before I even realized what we were doing, I suddenly heard the sound of the front door opening and then slamming shut. A second later Anna's father called her name. "I'm home, sweetie!" he added.

Anna and I sort of jumped apart. For a second all I could think about was how this was the second time in two days that an adult had interrupted when I was kissing someone.

But then I guess I started to recognize what

had just happened. And I had no idea how to deal with it. So I stood up and mumbled something about going home for dinner.

"Okay," Anna said. Her voice didn't sound too sad anymore. In fact, it was soft and sort of whispery. I'd never heard her talk like that before. "See you tomorrow, Salvador."

I bolted for the door, mumbling a quick "hello" to Mr. Wang before practically running down the walk.

Heights and Sights
Sweet Valley Tower by Moonlight
(revision)
by Elizabeth Wakefield

All of us have seen the lofty shape of the Sweet Valley Tower rising above our town like a beacon. But how many have actually ridden the elevator to the top and looked out over the twinkling lights of Sweet Valley by the light of the silvery moon? How many of us have gazed up at the stars above, seeming much closer than they do from the ground, and wished that we could read our future there as ancient astronomers once believed they could?

I visited our beloved tower recently, and it was a very thought-provoking experience. From its height I had a sweeping view of the town I've lived in all my life. Sweet Valley looks both familiar and strange from that new angle, and I saw many of the town's landmarks in a whole new light. It's funny how you can look at a building or park or house that you've visited hundreds of times, and suddenly it's like you've never even seen it before. You start to wonder—has the building actually changed? Or are you just noticing new things about it? It can really make you think.

In closing, I would recommend a visit to the Sweet Valley Tower to anyone who is looking for a new perspective on your hometown—or on life.

Elizabeth

I sighed and chewed on the end of my pencil as I read over what I'd just written. It was almost seven-thirty, and I had been working on rewriting my tower article ever since I'd excused myself from the dinner table half an hour earlier. I'd only managed to choke down a few bites of chicken, and Mom had asked me again and again if I felt all right.

No, I felt like saying. *My life is a mess. I don't know what I feel about anything anymore.*

But instead I'd just smiled and assured her that I'd had a really big lunch. Then I had locked myself in my room, sat down at my desk, and gotten to work.

Or tried to anyway. It hadn't been easy to concentrate. Every time I thought about the Sweet Valley Tower, it reminded me of Salvador. And every time I thought about Salvador, I wondered if we were doing the right thing. It had all seemed so logical when I was talking to him earlier. But now I didn't know what to think about any of it. I wasn't even sure how I felt about Salvador anymore. I mean, the way he'd reacted when I said we ought to cool it had really been kind of immature.

Still, I figured maybe he was just overcome with his own feelings. If he felt anywhere near the same way I did, that would explain a lot.

I read back over what I'd written for the new article. It sounded kind of stupid, but I was running out of ideas. The only other thing I could think to write was, *The Sweet Valley Tower is a very interesting place to visit. Especially if you bring along someone you want to kiss. Of course, it helps to leave all grandmothers at home unless you want to get interrupted and die of embarrassment.*

The thought of publishing something like that in *Zone* made me smile, at least a little. Pushing the article aside, I rested my chin on my hand and let my mind drift back to Salvador. I really wished we hadn't snapped at each other the way we had just before he ran off. But I tried not to worry about it too much.

Anyway, I thought, *it isn't as if we have to ignore our feelings forever. Just until Anna feels better and we can tell her the truth. Then Salvador and I can figure things out somehow.*

I shivered a little, imagining what might happen then. But before I could think too much about it, the phone rang. I hurried out into the hallway to pick it up, hoping it might be Salvador calling to report on how his visit with Anna had gone.

"Wakefield residence. Elizabeth speaking," I said automatically.

"Hi, Elizabeth. It's Anna."

Her voice was so soft, I could hardly hear her. "Anna?" I said. "Are you okay?"

"I think so." This time she sounded a little louder. "I think I'm really much better now. Um, that's sort of what I'm calling to tell you. I just had to tell someone what happened, and I didn't know who else to call."

"What happened?" I asked, wondering why she was calling me instead of Salvador, her best friend. Did he end up not going there after all?

"Salvador was here a little while ago," she said. I let out my breath, relaxing. "He stopped by, you know, to see how I was doing. It turns out he did remember about Tim." She laughed sheepishly. "I thought he'd totally forgotten. But he was really sweet when he came by."

I smiled, relieved that Salvador had done the right thing. "That's great, Anna," I said sincerely. "At a time like this it always helps to have friends you can count on."

"That's true," she agreed. "But that's not really what I'm trying to tell you."

"What is it?" I asked. I couldn't help noticing that her voice sounded kind of weird. Shaky, but not in a sad way. "What happened?"

She paused for a second, although I could still hear her breathing through the phone. I pressed the receiver to my ear, not wanting to miss a thing.

"Well," she said at last, "it's kind of hard to get out. But I'm just going to say it." She inhaled deeply. "You see, when he was here, Salvador—he—he kissed me."

For a second I wasn't sure I'd heard her right. "He what?"

She giggled. "Don't make me say it again," she pleaded. "It's too embarrassing. In a good way, of course," she added quickly. "But it's just—well, I didn't know he felt that way about me." She hesitated for a second. "Actually, well, I sort of thought he might still like you."

"Oh." I had no idea what else to say. My head was spinning like crazy. How could this be true? What was going on here? "Um, that's nice," I choked out at last. "I'm—I'm really happy for you, Anna."

"Thanks. At first I wasn't sure what to do," she admitted. "I mean, Salvador and I have been

127

friends for so long. I wouldn't want to mess that up or anything." She let out a happy little sigh. "But then I thought about it. And it's just so natural, you know? I mean, I think maybe it was meant to happen."

"Maybe," I agreed, feeling a little sick. I couldn't believe this was for real. How could Salvador have done this? Had I completely misjudged him? Did he actually care about either of us, or was he just goofing around with us both, not even realizing how his actions might be hurting other people?

Anna spoke again. "Somehow," she said shyly, "knowing that he cares about me—you know, *that* way—actually makes it a little easier to deal with all my thoughts about Tim."

"That's great, Anna," I said, trying to sound like I meant it. After all, I wasn't mad at *her*. She hadn't done anything wrong.

I knew for sure there was absolutely *no way* I was going to let Salvador see that it bothered me one bit.

If I ever decided to speak to him again, that is.

Jessica

The phone rang on the table beside the couch. "Aren't you going to answer that?" Steven asked lazily from his position lying on the rug in front of the TV. He tossed another potato chip in his mouth. He'd been stuffing his face nonstop for the past half hour, even though we'd just had dinner. I swear, that boy could eat an entire supermarket full of food in one day if Mom and Dad would let him. Incidentally, he was also the one who was forcing me to watch the idiotic kung fu movie. When I'd tried to change the channel to something normal, like MTV, he'd snatched the remote control away and stuck it under his butt. No way was I going after it.

The phone rang again. I shot it an irritated glance. It was the second time it had rung in the past ten minutes. Then I turned back to the TV. I was feeling kind of grumpy, mostly because Elizabeth had rushed off and locked herself in her room right after dinner, which meant I hadn't had a chance to beg her to go to that science lecture with Ronald tonight. I'd tried talking to her about it through the door, but she had ignored me, and I'd given up.

"Will you get it already?" I asked my brother. There was no way I was answering any ringing phones tonight. Not when Ronald Rheece might be lurking at the other end, begging me to come to that science lecture. I glanced at my watch. The lecture started in less than an hour. At least after that I would know I was safe—for a while anyway.

"Oh, sorry, Elizabeth," Steven said. "For a minute there, I thought you were Jessica. But I know you couldn't be her because she would never pass up the chance to blab on the phone with her friends for twelve or thirteen hours about the differences between lip gloss and lipstick."

I just rolled my eyes as the phone rang again, not bothering to dignify his stupid joke with a reply. "Somebody's got to answer that," I said, glancing at the phone. "Come on, Steven. Get it."

"Can't. Too comfortable." Steven lobbed another chip into his mouth.

I groaned as the next ring came. Mom and Dad had gone out for a walk, but I couldn't understand why Elizabeth wasn't picking up. Steven didn't move, except to grab another fist-ful of chips. His eyes were glued to the TV. At the next ring I finally gave in and grabbed the phone.

"Hello," I said in the lowest, deepest fake voice I could manage. "Wakefield residence."

"Um, hello?" a voice I didn't recognize replied. "Is—Is Elizabeth there?"

"Who's this?" I asked in my normal voice.

"It's Salvador," the voice replied, sounding a little confused. "Jessica?"

I rolled my eyes. "Yeah, it's me," I said. "Hold on, I'll go get her."

I dropped the phone on the table and raced for the stairs. "Elizabeth!" I bellowed at the top of my lungs. "Phone!"

A moment later she appeared at the top of the stairs. "Who is it?"

"Nobody good," I reported. "Just boring old El Salvador."

She frowned. "Oh. I don't want to talk to him."

I raised an eyebrow, surprised at her hostile tone. "What do you mean, you don't want to talk to him?"

"Which word didn't you understand?" Elizabeth snapped. "Just tell him I'm not here."

I shrugged. I wasn't about to beg her to

talk to a loser like El Salvador if she didn't want to. Of course, that didn't mean I wasn't a little curious about exactly *why* she didn't want to. . . .

I hurried back to the phone. "Hello?" I said. "El Salvador? She said to tell you she's not in."

"To *tell* me she's not there?" he asked. "What? Did you say it was me?"

I sighed impatiently. He was making even less sense than he usually did. "No, I told her it was the queen of England," I said sarcastically. "She said she didn't want to talk to you because she's not British."

"Whatever," Salvador muttered. "See you." He hung up before I could say anything else.

I hung up and headed for the stairs, planning to pound on Elizabeth's door until she gave up and let me in.

But I didn't have to. She was sitting on the top step, staring downstairs. When she saw me coming, she hopped up. "Oh!" she said, looking flustered. "What did you tell him?"

"You heard me," I pointed out. "You must have, if you were sitting there the whole time."

She scratched her ear. "I guess," she said. "So what did he say?"

"I don't know," I replied. "Nothing." I hurried up the stairs and peered at her face, which was all scrunched up. "Why? What's going on?"

"Nothing," she said quickly. Then she got up and rushed back to her room.

But I stayed right on her heels and darted in before she could lock me out. "Okay, Lizzie," I declared with my hands on my hips. "Spit it out. Did you and El Salvador have some kind of fight?"

"I don't want to talk about it," she muttered.

"Come on," I wheedled. "Tell me."

"No." Her eyes narrowed, and she pursed her lips together. But I could beat her at the stubbornness game any day.

"Tell me," I repeated, tapping my foot on the floor. *"Now."*

"Jessica, please. Leave me alone!" she said, sitting down at her desk and turning her back to me. "I'm busy."

I walked over and perched on the edge of her desk. "Too busy to talk to your very own twin?" I asked sweetly. "I don't think so. Now spill."

She frowned at me. "I told you. I don't want to talk about it."

"Come on," I said. "You know you're going to tell me eventually. You always do. So why not save us both some time and trouble?"

She glared at me. "Look, Jessica," she said.

"You know that science lecture you were bugging me about before?"

"Yes?" I said instantly. "What about it?"

She shrugged. "I wouldn't mind getting out of the house for a while," she said. "So if I agree to go, will you get off my back?"

"It's a deal!" I stuck out my hand and grabbed hers, pumping it up and down before she could change her mind. It wasn't like I really cared what she and her dorky friends were up to anyway. Besides, Elizabeth always told me everything eventually, whether I wanted to know or not. So this was definitely a win-win situation for me. "I'll go call Ronald. He'll be thrilled!"

I raced back to the phone and grabbed the phone book out of the drawer. Minutes later I was explaining everything to Ronald. He sounded pretty happy when I told him how Elizabeth was totally dying to go to the quark lecture with him. Of course, he had to be majorly depressed that I wasn't going, but he did a good job of hiding it. And once he got to know Elizabeth and realized the two of them had way more in common than he and I did, I would be free and clear. I couldn't wait.

After arranging for Ronald's parents to stop by and pick her up, I hurried back upstairs to give

Elizabeth the good news. Her door was locked again.

"Lizzie?" I said, knocking. "What are you doing? Ronald will be here to get you in half an hour."

"I'll be ready." Her voice sounded muffled. "I just want to fix my article first."

From inside the room, I thought I heard the sound of paper ripping. I shrugged. I didn't care what she did for the next half hour as long as she didn't back out on our deal. "Okay," I called back cheerfully. "But don't forget to wear something nice. I'm sure these quark lectures are pretty dressy occasions."

I headed back downstairs just in time to hear the phone ring again. This time I didn't hesitate to grab it. "Hello?" I sang out.

"Hi. It's Salvador again."

I snorted. "What is it this time?"

"I just wondered if you could ask Elizabeth if she'd please come to the phone," he said. "I really need to talk to her about something."

I definitely didn't have time for this. And there was no way I was going to risk having El Salvador drag Elizabeth off for some long, serious talk about their little magazine or something right before she was supposed to be sweeping Ronald off his feet.

Jessica

"I told you before," I snapped briskly. "She can't talk to you right now. So give it up already, okay?"

I slammed down the phone. Then I headed for the stairs again, whistling cheerfully. I'd just remembered how Ronald had complimented my new butterfly T-shirt the week before. Maybe I could convince Elizabeth to wear it tonight.

Love Among the Quarks

8:16 P.M.   Ronald arrives at the Wakefields'
               doorstep to pick up his date for the
               lecture. When he sees Elizabeth
               coming out (she is *not* wearing
               Jessica's butterfly T-shirt), he gets so
               flustered at how pretty she is that he
               trips over the front step. Elizabeth
               politely pretends not to notice.

8:25 P.M.   Ronald and Elizabeth arrive at the
               Sweet Valley University lecture hall.
               Ronald has reserved seats in the
               front row. He waves at everyone he
               knows, including the speaker.

8:30 P.M.   Jessica leans back on the couch as a
               new show comes on MTV, feeling
               very pleased with herself as she real-
               izes the lecture is starting right now.
               "I'm a total genius," she says out loud.
                   Steven shoots her a sour look from
               his spot on the floor. "Oh yeah?" he
               mutters. "What kind of genius hides
               the remote down her shirt?"

8:42 P.M.   While the speaker is explaining the
               importance of quarks in the quest
               for scientific knowledge, Ronald

suddenly lets out a huge yawn and stretches his arms above his head. "What's the matter?" Elizabeth whispers to him. "Are you bored?"

"Not at all," Ronald replies, casually lowering his left arm around Elizabeth's shoulders. "I could never be bored when I'm with you."

8:42:01 P.M. Elizabeth shoves Ronald's arm off. "What are you doing?" she hisses.

"Just trying to show you how I feel," Ronald replies, looking slightly hurt.

"Well, don't!" Elizabeth shoots back a little too loudly.

The quark lecturer gives them a dirty look.

9:56 P.M. After the lecture is over and Ronald has spent half an hour saying hello to everyone he knows and introducing Elizabeth as "my beautiful date, Elizabeth Wakefield," Elizabeth takes him aside.

"Listen, Ronald," she says gently. "We have to talk. . . ."

Heights and Sights:
Sweet Valley Tower by Moonlight
(2nd revision)
by Elizabeth Wakefield

All of us have seen the lofty shape of the Sweet Valley Tower rising above our town like a beacon. A lot of people seem to think that the sight of it looming up there in the moonlight is some sort of romantic thing. But what's so romantic about a huge pile of steel beams and concrete anyway? And why should a little moonlight make it seem any more dreamy? After all, moonlight is where werewolves supposedly come from. The moon has been accused of driving people mad. And if all we had was the moon for light, all the flowers and trees would shrivel up and die and the world would be barren and cold.

Besides, isn't all this emphasis on romance and moonlight kind of silly when you think about it? In this reporter's opinion, people are a little too hung up on romance these days. The world would be a much better place if people spent more of their time and energy on worthwhile things like helping others and less hanging around moonlit towers hoping for romance.

Overall, I would say that the Sweet Valley Tower is worth visiting. But only if you need to do research for a geography class or something. Otherwise you'd probably be better off just staying home and doing something useful.

Jessica

"Tell me you're joking, Elizabeth," I begged, clutching the back of the bus seat in front of me for support. "Please, just stop torturing me and tell me you're joking."

Elizabeth shot me a grumpy glance. "For the ninety-eighth time, I'm not joking, Jessica," she said. "You knew I didn't have any romantic interest in Ronald. Why did you make him think I did anyway?"

I felt like tearing out my hair. All my brilliant planning, totally ruined! "I can't believe you just came right out and told him you didn't like him that way." I moaned. "This is a disaster. A total, complete disaster."

"Why?" Elizabeth still looked annoyed. "What's the big deal? And once again, why did you tell Ronald that I liked him? It was pretty embarrassing when he brought it up." She made a face. "It's just lucky that he's such a nice guy, or it could have been really awkward."

"I had to tell him that," I said, sinking down

against the lumpy vinyl bus seat. There was no reason not to tell her the whole story now. Not when everything was already ruined. "He has a huge crush on me, and it was the only way I could think of to get him to forget about me." I shrugged. "You know, I figured since we look so much alike and you actually care about stuff like quarks . . ."

Elizabeth let out a short laugh of disbelief. "You're incredible, Jessica," she exclaimed. "Truly incredible."

"I know." I grabbed the seat again as the school bus rumbled over a pothole. "That's what got me into this situation in the first place."

Elizabeth just rolled her eyes and laughed again. Then she opened up her notebook and started scribbling away at her stupid *Zone* article again. She didn't say another word to me for the rest of the ride.

When we got to school, I was tempted to skip my locker again. But I really needed a textbook I'd left there, so I took a deep breath and headed over.

Ronald was there. Of course. That was just the way my luck was going that day. "Hi, Jessica!" he greeted me happily. "Hey, you really missed a great lecture last night."

"Bummer," I muttered, reaching into the

locker and rooting around in the mess of papers and books on my shelf.

He went on for a while longer about the lecture, blabbing about all the thrilling details of quark exploration or something. I don't know; I wasn't really listening.

"Jessica," he said at last, his voice getting a little more bashful. "I'm not sure if you're aware of this, but it turns out your sister doesn't like me like you said she did last night on the phone."

I forced a smile as I finally located the book I needed and pulled it out, almost causing an avalanche in the rest of the locker. "Well, Ronald, Elizabeth can be a little shy," I said. "You shouldn't necessarily give up all hope."

He shook his head. "No, no, she was quite clear," he said sadly. "It's too bad, really. I probably shouldn't admit this now, considering what she said, but I've had a bit of a crush on her since the beginning of the year. I mean, she's so smart and responsible and nice. Not to mention beautiful. And she really seems to care about the important things in life, like science and school."

I rolled my eyes. He and Elizabeth were two of a kind, all right.

"Anyway," Ronald went on, "I didn't want to

hurt your feelings—that's why I thought I'd ask you first." He blushed slightly. "Sorry, I know I wasn't exactly subtle. I'm pretty disappointed, but I guess it's better that I know where I stand with Elizabeth now."

"Yeah," I said, feeling a little confused. Ronald had liked Elizabeth since the beginning of the year? But what about his crush on *me?* "Too bad."

He shot me a quick glance. "Oh, she was really nice about it, though," he said. "I mean, the way she said it almost made me like her more, you know?" He sighed and gazed at me. "Actually, I can't imagine finding another girl like her. . . ."

His voice trailed off, and for a second I wasn't sure why. Maybe because I wasn't paying that much attention. But he continued to gaze at me thoughtfully, and a very disturbing gleam came into his eyes.

Uh-oh. I gulped, finally figuring out what was happening here. How could I have been so stupid? Such a total, absolute, hopeless moron? *Ronald didn't have a crush on me before,* I thought desperately. *He was just grateful for that stupid dollar and trying to be friendly in his own geeky way. Concerned in a locker-partner kind of way about that fake rash and the rest of it. And, of* course, trying to use me to get to know Elizabeth better.

I gulped again. Ronald was smiling now. A new, extra-bright, definitely adoring smile. I backed away, clutching my books to my chest.

So what did I do? I set him up with Elizabeth, I thought. I encouraged him to like my sister. My identical twin sister. And when he found out she didn't like him back and started looking around for a substitute . . .

"So, Jessica," Ronald said, leaning toward me so close that I could almost smell the minty freshness of his toothpaste, "Can I walk you to class?"

A n n a

As I walked toward school, I felt calmer and happier than I'd felt in ages. I mean, part of me—a *big* part of me—was still so over-whelmed with sadness that I sometimes thought I couldn't possibly stand it for one more second. But at least now there was another part, a warm, safe, special part, that felt like life just might be worth living after all.

It was still hard to believe what had hap-pened between Salvador and me. After all these years of friendship, it felt weird to take this step. And kind of scary too.

I was almost at the school grounds when I spotted Salvador. He was walking down the sidewalk ahead of me, his hands shoved in his pockets and his head sort of tipped forward, like he was checking to make sure he wasn't stepping on any cracks.

Normally I would have run up behind him and tripped him, to get back at him for doing the same thing to me so many times. Or maybe

I would have started throwing the grapes from my lunch at him. Or just jogged up to him and started talking.

But somehow none of those things seemed quite like the right thing to do now. Instead I just picked up my pace until I caught up and was walking beside him.

"Hi," I said, a little breathless from hurrying. "How are you?"

That sounded kind of weird. It wasn't the type of thing we usually said to each other. But Salvador didn't rag on me for it. Instead he smiled politely. "I'm fine," he answered. "How are you?"

"Fine." I didn't know what I was supposed to say next, so we just walked along silently for a few steps. Then I cleared my throat. "Hey, we have that algebra quiz today, right? Did you study?"

"No." Salvador shrugged. "I guess I forgot about it. Did you study?"

"Not really."

We walked along without talking again. I was kind of glad we were almost to the school doors. I hadn't expected things to be so awkward between us.

It's okay, though, I told myself as we cut across the patchy little lawn in front of the school building. *I mean, it's only natural for us to feel a little strange with each other at first. After all, this is a pretty major change. I'm sure things will get back to normal. We just need some time to get used to it.*

"I'd better go," Salvador said as we walked into the school. "My history teacher wants to talk to me before classes start."

"Okay. Um, see you later." I reached out quickly and sort of tapped him on the arm. It wasn't exactly a huge public display of affection or anything, but he blushed a little. So did I, I guess. But touching him felt . . . nice.

Yep, all we need is a little time, I thought as I hurried away toward my locker. *To get used to the idea that we're a couple now.* I hugged my books to my chest, grinning at the thought. *And soon,* I added to myself, *everything will be perfect!*

Salvador

I couldn't believe the mess I'd made. I really couldn't believe it. Even for me, this was major.

I turned and paused, watching Anna hurrying off down the hall toward her locker. She was walking so quickly and lightly that she was practically skipping.

"I'm such an idiot," I muttered. Some girl I didn't know heard me talking to myself and gave me a weird look, but I didn't even care. My life was totally ruined anyway. And it was my own stupid fault.

What had I been thinking yesterday? What in the world had made me kiss Anna? I didn't think of her that way. I'd never thought of her that way. There was only one girl I *did* think of that way, and that was Elizabeth.

But what was I supposed to do about it now? It didn't matter if I didn't want Anna as a girlfriend. She obviously wanted me—and if I told her the truth about me and Elizabeth,

I'd definitely lose her friendship for good.

There's no way I can explain it to her so she won't hate me, I thought helplessly. *Especially not when she's right in the middle of the whole Tim thing.*

It all seemed so mixed up and hopeless all of a sudden that I couldn't take it anymore. I pressed the palms of my hands against both eyes so hard that I saw sparks on the backs of my eyelids. I felt horrible. I was trapped in my own impossible web of incredible stupidity. The person who had been my best friend for eight years thought she was my girlfriend. And the girl I wanted to be my girlfriend wouldn't even come to the phone when I called.

When I finally took my hands away from my eyes, I saw that two other girls were now staring at me like I was nuts.

Then I saw Elizabeth. She was walking down the hall toward me, carrying a couple of books and a brown paper lunch bag. She looked just as beautiful as always. But her pretty eyes were blazing with anger, and her normally smiling mouth was pulled together in a tight frown.

"Elizabeth," I said as we reached each other. "I—"

I didn't have a chance to say anything more.

She didn't even slow down. Just nodded at me coolly and swept on past.

I spun around, watching her go with a sinking heart, knowing that things were even worse than I'd thought. That my whole world was collapsing around me.

And I had no idea what to do about it.

Check out the **all-new** ....

(Sweet Valley Web site—

www.sweetvalley.com

New Features

Cool Prizes

The **ONLY** official Web site!

Hot Links

(And much more!)

BFYR 217

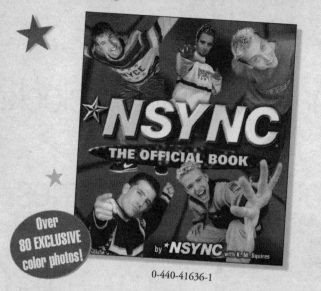